Thin Ice Zombies In LA Nowhere to Run or Hide! Returns!

Jean Marie Rusin

Edited by K Downing

authorHOUSE®

AuthorHouse™
1663 Liberty Drive
Bloomington, IN 47403
www.authorhouse.com
Phone: 1-800-839-8640

First published by AuthorHouse 8/22/2011

ISBN: 978-1-4634-4731-1 (sc)

Printed in the United States of America

Any people depicted in stock imagery provided by Thinkstock are models, and such images are being used for illustrative purposes only. Certain stock imagery © Thinkstock.

This book is printed on acid-free paper.

Table of Contents

QUARATINE

Others books by Jean Marie Rusin

A Polish Christmas story with a Magical Christmas tree
Spooky
Willow Lakes Haunitngs!
Mysterious Nights Séance Ghostly Hauntings!
Nights of Terrors!
A Drama Queen Collides with Prince Charming!
No Ending Dreams!
No Ending Dreams! (The Reunion)
Thin Ice Zombies In LA Nowhere to runs or hide!
Mystery Man

"Silent Nothing"

Zombies walks the street of Los Angeles and Hawaii, Special Report, warning stay inside and close the doors and windows, wait until help arrives, then breaking news, a thousand zombies spotted at the North Shore, there was a attack and you sees guts and bloods and bodies broken apart. Zombies are everywhere and watched out, I looked out of the window and I said to Jim, when we are we going to the helicopter and fly away from here and maybe, we can even get to New York, and we will tried tonight said Jim to Kelly, ok! I will pack the things, and we need to gets to the car, and but we are surrounded, I know but we need to get to the car and drive to the airport and get out of here but the news said that we need to locked up everything and stay for help!

Kelly said to Jim I don't wants to die here because of staying we need to get out now, fine. Don't you those black crows, on the tree and the zombies not too far from we need to drive much faster, they are getting closer to us, and then the car stall and I asked what happened well we are out of gas, and need to get out of car and find a place because and not to be seen. That night we ran into the wood and we saw that house and then I realize we would back at the cabin, and they would coming closer, at moment we step inside grab a table cross the door and then we need to sees to check the doors and windows.

Kelly and Jim, sat in the dark, then there sounds and banged and banged and then the window broke... zombies, then somehow one zombie got inside and Jim got up and took a stick and hit the zombie, but zombie got up and tried to my arm, and Kelly took the stick.. And hit the zombies on the head. The zombie fell down and the zombie was dead.

Kelly ran to Jim did you get bitten and she looked at his hand and he was fine, but we need to get help, and we cannot stay here neither.

If we stay we will dies here, so we need find a place and we cannot stay in the woods in the cabin they are out there so we need to leaves now and we need to fight them off and but there are thousand of them and we don't have a gun and have no weapons, and there is no one to save us. I know what you are saying but we need to get into the car and go far away from here do you understand? Yes I do so let do it and don't whine.

So they we will be fine and don't get bitten, I will tried not too.

When I says runs you runs has fast has you can, and I will be in back of you. I will always keep you safe, you promise, yes I do.

Jim and Kelly decided to attempt the second times and they ran so quick and Kelly started up the car and they drove off and they were be follows by the "ZOMBIES" and they are catching up to us.. Just keep on driving and keep your eyes on the road, I am.

About a minute later, the car stalls and said I said we are out of gas no it cannot be happening again! We need to find others survivors, ok we will and don't worry and they got out of the car and they walks for miles and miles and they reach the highway and they saw car smash and bodies everywhere. Kelly said to Jim we need to find shelter and gets away from them they are coming, I cannot runs and Kelly said I am tired but you need to gets up and don't end up becoming zombies.

Ok! I am coming and wait for me said Kelly.

Come on Kelly! All right but I am hungry and tired and I want to go home and we are not going home, because of the chemical spills and we cannot get infection just keep on moving all right!

Don't stop, if you do you will get infection I will shoot you in the head and I will have to be alone and I don't want that so let keeps on moving and try to make it through the night, then we might we lucky! What are you talking about I am going to died and we will find a safe place to stay until the military comes and take us there. You don't know what going to happen to us and we can end up being dead meat and your right!

Later that night Kelly and Jim hid in the woods until morning but they knew that they were not clear from the zombies.

Now what? I don't know but we can just stand here, we will get killed.

No we are going now!

They ran for hours and hours and they saw a bridge and Jim said let's cross the bridge, are sure, yes so let go and we will be in town and safe.

Kelly follows Jim and they walks into and it was quiet and not a soul.

Mores Jim and Kelly, walks toward the café and they walks inside and no one here, that what they thought.

About a second later, … the zombies were walking toward Kelly and Jim said don't get bit, and I won't and I will not get infection and turn into a zombies so we need to get out of this café and find a safe place to stay I do agree with you Jim but we are out of gas and we cannot walks alls the ways to the highway because the zombies will eat us up so what is the solution but time is running out and we need to do now because we will end up being dead meat, I know but I am surrounded and we need to do a distract to gets away and ok! They are getting closer to me and I am afraid Jim so do something now! Then Kelly said well, well soon I will become one of them and you will be dead too.

Then he somehow grab Kelly through the zombies and got her out of the café and they were outside but they still were surrounded by the zombies and now, they had to runs for there lives.

Then Kelly fell between two zombies were about to bite her hand, and Jim find a gun and shot it in the head and pick up Kelly and ran and ran for hours and then they stop in the end of the street and thousand of zombies were coming closer and now Kelly and Jim said we need to find a place to stay until morning and then we will have a chance to lives.

Then Kelly said we need to make love and before we died, and Jim said no ways we are going to make it and don't have no doubt about that's!

A Sunny day in the sun

It was a next day for Kelly and Jim and they somehow reach the beach and Kelly said well let lies in the sun and I think that we will be safe and Jim said I don't that is such a good idea, said Jim.

Jim you worry too much! We make so far but we will be fine!

So far we do not sees any "zombies" and we can stay here for a while.

Then later afternoon, it was going dark and we should leaves now you right so I will gets the car but you are not leaving me here alone!

So Kelly and Jim would walk to the car and from no where Kelly spotted the zombies coming toward them. Jim said what are we going to do now? Get into the car and drive fast to the main street and called for help, I think that is a bad ideas, the zombies will be more in the city so we should go to the countryside and go toward the military and we will be safe, are sure and we wont gets shot by the soldiers? I don't know but we need to leave now. So they drove off for miles and miles and then the car stops and Jim said why did you stops, we are out of gas, you must be kidding, am I smiling, no and we will be dead meats if we don't move now. Ok! Kelly said why don't we go toward the hills and walks to that house and yes you are right! They walks up the hills and they saw thousand of zombies coming toward them and now runs for your life and don't look back and then we got to cross road and Jim said why don't we take the left road and it will lead us to the lakes. I believe that we will be safe and away from zombies.

Once again they walks for miles and miles and tired and hungry and then Kelly sat down and Jim said get up it really getting dark and we need to move and found shelter for the night, fine and Kelly got up and they walks toward the cottage and it was clear and they walks inside and they lock the door and also locked the windows and now we will be safe and then Kelly said I hears sound it is coming from the basement, and they someone is walking up stairs and Jim was about to hit that person and it was Joe and Joe said I thought that zombies were coming in and I was about to shoot you and your friends, and Jim said is the basement secure and Joe said yes it is and we will be safe here and no sighting of "Zombies" so far and I think we will be safe. Then Joe said do you have a car and Jim said yes but out of gas, that is not good! We need a backup plan, do you have a gun? But only few bullets, and there are thousand of them out there! Then Joe said did zombies bite you? No! Good because if you were you would be infection and then we would have too shot you in the head, ok!

But when you shoot them just in the head and they will die.

About one hour later, Joe said, the zombies probably follow you and Jim said why? Looks outside, oh my god! Then Kelly said what are we going to do? But be quiet and just sit and we will be fine, then Jim said they are coming toward the door, no! Gets some woods. Ok and hammer it good on the door and it will keep them out.

Will it be strong enough to keeps them, out? Not sure but I hope it does and so we might be safe tonight! About tomorrow well let worry about tonight and not tomorrow, so you are saying that we might end up being dead meat, no thanks! I didn't sign for this…

Ok I didn't neither and so I wish that we didn't comes here, but I trusted you and now we have to fight off the zombies and I don't know if I am strong enough to do it? Yes you are and don't says that you are not! But hurried don't let them catch you and we will be safe and we will not end being zombies, are sure, there so many of them…

They are catching up and if I do gets bitten shoot me in the head and don't think about it and just killed me, and promise me, ok do the same for me, sure I will! One more day they survive the zombies and didn't get bitten or end up dead and still fighting off the living dead and still no help is coming and the bullets are running out and a place to stay and now running out of foods and then Kelly said what will happened to us if we will be save, I don't have a answer for that's!

About two hours later and they heard helicopter above there head and a lot shooting and then they heard that the zombies were coming to the cottage and now Kelly what are we going to do now? I am thinking but we are only have five bullets and there are thousand out there and I know.

Are we going to gets rescue by someone I hope soon!

Jim I am really so scare and I am, but we need to leave here and but we are on an island and now we need to find a boat and sail away from here! But the zombies are there and how are we going back to our boat and get to the helicopter and fly way from here, but I was wrong taking us here, I think that you are right! Don't agree with me, please we have a delicate situation and we don't have a way out and just being foods for the zombies and I refuse to give up at this time. Me too!

So now we need to distract the zombies and then runs for your life to the boat and leave this island of zombies.

Who will distract the zombies and Jim said I will and what happened if you get bitten and eat up by the zombies and I will be alone. I know but you need to tell the story what happened and I don't like this.

I don't neither but we have no choice so when you reach the boat and then start up the motor and just leave and I am not leaving you here, if I get the infection, I will become the night of the living dead and you will have too shoot me dead.

I do understand but I am going to wait for you and you will not get infection and Jim said come on to reality. I am I know that you will be ok!

You really don't know but time is ticking and I need to do that now.

Fine! Soon have I made the noises and you move fast toward the boat.

Time running out

Kelly got to the boat and was looking at the beach and Jim was not coming yet! At that moment I started up the boat and then I saw Jim coming toward me and I called out and said " Looks behind you" but he didn't sees that there were about five zombies coming toward him and at that moment I was slight moving, and then Jim was grab and I decided to jump out of the boat and I took a stick and hit them over and one grab my arm and was about to bite me and then Jim started to fight and fight and that was the last one and Jim said that was a close one and then they both on the boat and they thought, they were safe but somehow one zombie got on the boat and at that moment I thought that Jim was going to be dead meat and I somehow took the stick and hit it over the head and fell into the water and then I notice there were more zombies swimming toward the boat and I said to Jim we need to get on dry land and get on the helicopter and leave this place immediately.

Yes I agree but we are still in the middle of the ocean and the wave are getting really wild and shaking and I know, I know that we will be fine!

Sure, I like that you are being positive about our situation.

So I see the island and went we get there we will be fine, went they got to the island and tied up the boat and walk on the sand and toward the woods, and they stop they looking into each other eyes, then they make love and they got up and walk toward the cabin..

Kelly and Jim, walk toward the door and opened up and went inside and close door.

Then he grabs her and said if this the last time and I want to make love to you again! Yes I want the same and they got close and Kelly said, I heard sound and voices and Jim said it must be winds, no I think we have zombies out there! No, I don't want to die here. We will be safe.

About one hour later, they were banged, at the door and they broke in and they were walking inside and Kelly and Jim. Meanwhile they were in the basement and they thought they be fine but then they were coming from alls different direction and now Kelly said for sure we are going to be goner, don't says that, we will get out here, well you don't have bullets and looks how many are here and then when she spoke she heard gun fire and then Joe came inside the basement and said I have a car and we need to leaves here immediately and Kelly said fine, and Jim said we will not be safe out there! Well you not safe in here so take a chance and get out of here now…

About five minutes later they walks outside and the zombies were coming toward them and then Joe started to shoot them in the head and then they got inside the car and drove very quickly and they were following them and Kelly said "we cannot escape them" yes we can!

Kelly got very close to Jim and holds him tight and then they were out of the woods and they were headed to Los Angeles, and Kelly said that is not a good idea to go there! Well we will have more peoples to help us out and they also have a place that we can stay and we will be protection from the zombies, so why are you here? Well I am looking for Valerie and she was not in LA so she left the shelter and I need to find her.

So we might get caught by zombies and we will walks like the "Night of the living dead".

No, it not going to happened. Are you sure? Yes, you are not god! I know but I do know the road so we will be fine. I don't want to end up dead.

Two hours later they arrive and we were in LA and Kelly said to Jim and Joe, I cannot wait to sees my friend Lisa. She is probably dead, don't says that's! Ok but it could be true. I don't want to listen to this.

Joe and Kelly were talking about there future about there and Joe said don't plan it, and Kelly said why? The world is chaos, I know that but I do want to be his wife, but who will marry you? A zombie's priest or minister?

There must be someone would marry us , they were wandering stop at the justice of the peace, well he could be a zombies, and why are you go negative, and so need take our times and we will have the safe location and are you sure and you are not taking us into trap? I could have left us in the woods, why do you dislike me so much! I just don't trust you; I don't trust you or your boyfriend. But why were you in the woods in the first place just a getaway! Then we heard the "special report" about the dead coming back to lives.

So have been bitten? I need to know. No we have not about you? No!

Then Kelly said I need to rest, well I guess you want to be dead meat. No I don't I just need to sit a while, and I feel a bit shaking, and Jim hold Kelly and Joe said soon we will be in LA and I will looks for Lisa at her place and then if we cannot take her to the safe heaven.

Then Kelly said this place is quiet and dessert and I think we will be all ready. When she said that then Zombies were coming out of the alley and then stop and said Joe where did they come from?

There was a chemical spill in the lab and some were infection and so it spread very quickly and no control.

They are going closer and just runs and don't looks, they are getting very close, don't stop and then Kelly fell down and Joe pick her up and Jim was ahead and didn't stop running to got to the apartment and when they enter she was one of them. No! at that moment she was about to bite him, so Kelly push him away and put a stick into her head and she fell on the ground and some blood spill on Kelly face and when into the bathroom and wash her face and said I am fine, do you have any cuts on your hands? No! You will be fine.

Then Jim said you took a risk and to save us and I don't want you to become a zombie.

Survive days

We need to leave now and find that shelter now, I do understand but it is on the other side of town, and it will be a little difficult to get there!

I don't understand Joe, well we will need to go to the dock and take a boat and get way on do you understand? Yes!

Ok, we will go around the building through the alley and then get the end of the street and then get into the building and gets what we need and then we can travel further away from, I believe that LA is not the place to stay so we need to go to "New York City" but that is about 3, 000 miles away and I don't know if we are going to make out from.

We need to go now, we will be able to be safe here anymore so let move fast ... so we have a long times to gets there.

I know we don't have the any guns or bullets and we need to move fast.

Then Kelly said they getting closer and closer, I don't if we going to make it, they are gained up and they are so closed that they will catch us and I don't want to die. We will not died I promise you.

But you don't know that and anything can happen and you cannot predict the future can you, no I cannot so. Why suddenly you want to bite my head off and I don't just wants to live like you do. Now we need on moving and until we will be safe, ok! Joe and Kelly and Jim walks for miles and miles and they got to a town and it was not invaded my zombies, but it was really quiet and Kelly said I really don't like this place and I wants to leaves, we will be safe here and how do you know? I don't but I feel a bad feeling about this place I don't understand?

I have a feeling that someone is watching us and I don't want to stay.

Well you are just imagination going wild and I think that we should stay.

Fine! But if I am right we still can end up dead and I don't like this.

One of us will stay up and keeps watched and then the morning we can leave, but it is possible that we still end being dead. Don't say that Kelly I don't want to hear that! Kelly when on the couch and close her eyes and fell asleep and then Jim said I will go to bed and Joe said don't worry and we will be fine!

Later that night, Joe got up from the chair the and looks outside and he couldn't believe his eyes and then he woke up Joe and said Looks!

I cannot believe what I am seeing, witches flying over the building and children with coming into the door and Joe and said Jim let lock the door and stay quiet, and I am.

Then suddenly Kelly woke up and said what going on?

Be quiet they are trying to comes inside and I don't want to be caught by them, they might be children zombies.

But they don't look like zombies how can you tell? I don't!

About ten minute later, somehow one got inside and chasing us around the room and then almost caught Joe.

Kelly said Joe don't get caught. We need to find weapons, and then I don't believe that I am seeing witches and little children want to bite you.

But I told you this town was strange and I told you needed to leave and you didn't listen to me.

Stop it! Ok! I want to leaves now, but we cannot go we will be surrounded and the witches are controlling them.

I could be wrong, they can be vampires, and no I cannot handle this with zombies and vampire at the same times.

I heard that with vampires you need to stake them and with holy water, but with zombies, need to blow there head off and then they are dead.

Really how do we get way from here? The same way that we came in, and then we move very fast and runs for your life.

So is everyone ready to move and run from this place and get the hell out of town.

Yes we are, so you first why can you? Ok! Meet me at the end of road and then we will headed north on the path and head east near the meadow. Then we will go toward the highway and we will be safe.

So Joe ran out and he almost slip to the ground and he kept on running and saw that it was clear and he called out to Kelly and Jim and said it is ok to go and Kelly said I don't feel right about going.

Now you want to stay? Yes! But Joe is risking his life because of you.

I did wants to get way but there is a lot of danger than being here, we need him to come back, but he will be able to do so.

What are you saying? Well if he step out of the zone, it will not let him back,, you are saying crazy, but I know about the urban legend.

Not about vampires and zombies, but they don't somehow connect.

I am going to take him, no you will get slaughter and I don't want to lose you.

We can stay here neither and what is possession you to stay nothing.

I am just thinking about our survive and we will live don't you understand?

Yes, meanwhile Joe was running and running for his life and he stop and thought he was safe and he sat for a while and then something grab him and drag him way.

Jim said to Kelly he probably he made it and then Kelly said I don't think so, why are you saying that's!

Kelly suddenly got up and said well we need to leave before the full moon. But why? The dead will comes and we will be dead and we will roam the earth.

Before midnight we take the road that lead us out of here and follow the stars, you are sounding weird. But those are tales that I heard in the past and that is the only ways out to lives.

Each path we take will takes us different directions. Ok so now listen to me carefully we cannot stops just be very quiet.

No ways out

Jim was walking out of town with Kelly and then they notice they were back in the same place that they started and what going on here?

The town doesn't want us to leave and so we have a slight problem, Jim.

You were the one told us to that we could stay for a while and now we cannot leaves. Well I will figure out something!

But what, I don't understand, I thought the zombies were bad but now we have to deal with zombies, and then with witches and demons.

They walking toward us, now what? Runs and hide and don't let him gets catch us, we will be dead meat. No, don't let back.

I am trying to catch up but I am getting tired and hungry and I don't do this we need to be safe and not being hunting by zombies, so you called them zombies vampires, and they are not the ordinary zombies, they need brain and blood to survive and these are more vicious and more powerful, you don't says? Well why we are standing around let go fast ok!

Those zombies they can fly and walks so fast and catching up so let inside that house, and they step inside and someone said welcome! It was a vampire in the cape, now what? Kelly said Jim looks he is coming close to us and now he going to bite us so find a stake and he will be dead.

Hope that you are right so looks at his face and he is a vampire but he also looked like a zombie in his eyes and face, I don't know what to do?

They do looks like "zombies "but they are not the same bred, what do you means? Well these zombies are after blood and they also wants your brains, and if they bite you, you will instantly become a vampire and died and then they comes back and bite you again and you turned into a

13

Vampire / zombies and that is the worst, neither when your dead and you still becoming a zombies and I don't wants to be the undead.

I agree, Jim, and I don't want that so how to we killed them and I think first to shoot them in the head and then stake them.

Then Jim said ok we can rest for a while and then I will find a place to eat but not eaten by the undead, great! I didn't know that we were going to have this time of vacation when we left New York City.

Now I think that was the wrong that we went to Los Angeles and now we need to find shelter and a safe house from the zombies.

But we cannot control it so we only have to make it, I know but I can walks anymore but you need to a few more miles and we should be safe, and suddenly a quick car came and then stop and said so do you wants a ride to town and Kelly said sure we do! But Jim nodded his head and said no thanks! Then they took off and Kelly was angry at him and said we didn't have says no to them.

We could be in a town and safe, and then Jim explains and said you really didn't looked into there eyes, what do you means?

They were more aggressive zombies that drive and they also were part vamp. No you must be kidding?

Do you seeing me laughing? No! I am totally serious, Kelly.

Now what? They know that we are here and they probably comes back to gets us, your probably right so we need to gets off the road and hide in the woods for tonight, and sees if it clear to travel in the morning.

Then there is an other ways that they might not notice that we were alive, and I will pray to make it safe to wherever we be.

Kelly called out and said they are coming back and we need to hide now, they want to eat us up.

The car when by and then they saw the farm and Kelly said that we can go there and then we can stay overnight and then leave in the morning and then Kelly said I sees chickens and eggs and we can eat something and Jim said they can be infection and we can turned into zombies, so what do we eat and lives? I don't know Kelly, but I feel a chill, are you sick?

Have you been bitten? I don't know Kelly! Then Jim sat down and fell asleep, and Kelly tried to wake him up but he didn't wake up.

In few minute he woke up and he had fluid coming out of his mouth and Kelly said what wrong with you? But he didn't answer.

Now he was coming toward her and then was about to bite her and Kelly got up and ran to the barn door and screams, and Jim said what wrong?

I thought you became a zombies, and Kelly looked into his eyes and then you are one of them, and he got closer to her and then she hit him over the head and then she looked outside and she was surrounded by zombies and now Jim was about to bite her hand, and she pull it away.

Jim said runs Kelly, you cannot save me but save yourself.

Then Jim said Kelly take that stake and hit my head and into my brain and I will be dead, Jim no, I cannot! I will bite you and we both will become zombies, so do you wants to roam the earth that ways?

No, just do it now, before it is too late. I will always remember you and I will tell your family what happened. But they probably dead and I have no one, and you think the same about mine? It is a thin chance that they survive the zombies invaded. Do it now, bye my friend, I will miss you but you are wasting time, in any second I will turned on you and you will be a zombie. Now I will hit your head hard and into your skull and you will bleed.

Kelly got closer to Jim and was about to do it and the Police arrives and said Miss what are you doing and then they approach Jim and he bitten them and Kelly ran for her life and didn't looked back.

About one hour later, Kelly was In Arizona and she was walking on the highway and her Phoenix and she thought she was safe, but now Jim was an undead and the police and Kelly was hungry and Kelly walks into the restaurant and sat down and thought what to do next?

Alone

Kelly sat in the restaurant and then a waitress came up to her and said what do you wants to order Miss? Black coffee that alls for right now.

Then more peoples were coming in and Kelly feel uncomfortable about being there and then she got up and the waitress said where are you going? Too use the restroom and clean up a bit.

Ok! I felt that I been watched and I didn't like it not at alls.

That moment I watched the waitress and I thought she bought coffee and I looked at the coffee and it looked like blood, and at that moment I didn't know what to do to drink it or walks out but I was afraid.

I got up and I stood in the middle diner and the waitress ran over and said miss you don't like the coffee and I said I need some fresh air, and the waitress and you cannot go out in the dark, and I said is it night? I looked out and I said ok I will have the seat and the lights started to flicker and I called out and now I was alone and no one was there and now what?

About a minute later, I saw the zombies walking the streets and the waitress came over and said, child if you step out you will be there meal.

At that moment I just when back to the table and sat down and didn't look back but I will help you out and you will not be harm.

Two hours later, the waitress came out and said are you ready to come with me and I said where are we going? Just be quiet and you will be able to leave without the elders noticing you missing you, you are in danger they bought you here, what? I don't understand?

Follow me to the cellar and I didn't know what going to happened to me at that point, so I follow her and she took me to the outdoor about five miles away from town and she told me follow the path and not the woods and you will be headed south and then north, so I did listens and I was also afraid about what might happened to me?

When I was headed south and it was peaceful and quiet and no sounds of the undead and no elder and demons that wants to possession me.

But I stop when I turn north and I saw a shine particle and I pick it up and then I fell down and woke up and I was not dreaming, and I saw Jim and Joe and they told me to leaves but I felt that I couldn't move at that moment, and then I suddenly got up and ran and ran for hours and hours and then I got to house with a fence and it looked quiet and not invaded by zombies and the undead.

I when up to the door and I walks in and I sat down and I felt a sleep and the next morning the wind woke me up and I got up took a shower and I felt was alone and no one to speak too and didn't know what was going on in the world and then I when into the kitchen and then I screams!

I saw a dead body torn apart and blood and stains.

Then I ran out of the room and to the outside and I ran into Jon and he said where are you going? I am leaving this place, you have a dead person on the floor, oh you meant the "Zombie" it didn't looked like one and it looked like it was a person that you murder.

But miss you are wrong the zombie, try to bite me last night so I killed it.

I don't know you and I am leaving, and where are you going? None of your business, fine! So let the zombies eat you up and I have warns you!

Just go I don't care what happen to me. You should you need to spread the word about the zombies and you need to find a safe heaven and warns everyone it going to be doom day and you mean the end of the world. I am not sure. But you need to find a place to be safe and but also spread the word and make sure that you are not only survive of this infection, and hope that you gets away and make sure that you don't get caught by the vampire / zombies, you will end up twice dead, what? If you gets bitten by the zombie, you died and then if it bite you again, you wants blood and brain and you have no control and how do you know about this, and then she said looked into my eyes and you will sees you I am! No you are one of them and you didn't hurt me, because I didn't believe in killing when I was alive and so I tried to be strong, but Kate, then Kate said go now, I have the surge to bite you, and I ran from her and I didn't stop, but Kate told me not to be seen on the min road and not in the woods neither and so it was a tough journey to take.

Sure I make a few stops on the ways but I knew that I needed to travels further away and not be caught by the undead creature.

Then I stop and I saw a car and I thought it were be easier to travel by car and then I would end up in New York city and sees if my family is still alive.

But I was not sure, how it going to be and there were a lot of bad peoples that rob and killed for some foods and water and I was about to gets caught by them neither. I just kept driving in the near the woods and then I went on the highway and I knew some ways I needed to take a risk.

At that moment I stop because I was out of gas and I had one hundred fifty miles to go and now I was getting stressed out and I feel like that moment I was going to past out but I didn't and I when to the pump and filled up the tank with gas and I when inside to leave some money but it was empty I thought and then that creature come out from the back and started to chase me and I ran toward the door and when to the car and started up and I drove away and I didn't looked back, and about half hour later, I saw them roaming the road and I didn't know what to do?

I couldn't stop but I didn't want to get stuck and surrounded so I turns the car around and then I drove back where I came from and then I saw a dirt road and I enter and I knew it were be risking but at that time I took a chance and I kept on going and I reach the end and I saw the highway to route 86 and I went on it and drove very quickly and I reach, almost my destiny, but I was not out of the woods yet!

I knew that I was getting closer to New York City and I knew that were have cross the bridge to Harlem, and at that moment I just stops!

Trap on the bridge

At that moment I couldn't turned around the car and I knew that I had to cross the bridge but without a weapon and it were be suicide, and I were be probably end up being dead and I thought and thought for a minute and I knew that I probably get out the car or just take my chances, and then I heard some shooting and a men with a white jeep drove up and said get in and I will take you too safety, can I trust you? Well you really don't have a choice at this moment, but if you want to be dead meat be my guest, ok! I will go with you and then they shoot about fifty zombies and more were coming and they said My name is Mike and Mark, Steve, and Leo, and I am Kelly, and nice too meet you under this circumstance.

But Kelly you will be fine, and then they reach the mall and she said we are going to stay in the mall? Is it safe, so far it is?

So they enter the garage and it looked clear, and they drove to the higher level. They won't come and gets us? I don't know Kelly.

But they do smell us and they probably reach top floor but we are not in danger yet! So if they do come do you have a plan, no I don't.

We need to have an escape plan. They alls agree and said, for tonight we will be fine said Mike. Kelly I hope so, but they are making sound and they are saying they wants Brains, then Mark said they break through the glass door and they are in and how what? We are still ok here! Are you sure?

Are you monitoring the cameras and sees where they are heading?

Yes I am doing worry! But Kelly said we should be, they are advance zombies and they are much quicker than the ordinary zombies, so Kelly how do you the knowledge of the zombies, well my friend and I when through a lot and he got killed and he was called Joe and Jim, and they were my best friend, and I got warns by Kate, and she was a zombie/vampire but she left me go and she told me not to trust anyone.

But you came along and save me on the bridge, and I am here.

I think you will protection me and I will not get killed.

Mike said do you know how to shoot a gun? No! But I am willing to learn. So you are not afraid? Yes I am very afraid but I do wants to survive, us too. Mark ran inside and said they are on the second floor and they broke in, and some of them are going on the elevator, and that is not good, now we need a plan to escape but we do have a fire escape on the building and then we can reach the bottom but there will be zombies too, we need to find the same ways in and out.

But there a flaw in the plan, but we have no choice, I know that Kelly.

Mark once again ran into the roof and said they are coming nearer and soon they will be on the roof and then what?

Get ready too shoot and runs, and follows me when I get to the ladder to go down, ok! I am in back of us and we will go into the next floor down and tired to reach the garage and get to the car and drive away.

Mark and Leo said that is the plan so who stayed back and shoot them, any volunteers, no I am going and then Mike took out the gun and pointed the gun toward Mark and Leo, and said you too will fight off the zombies, about you, I will watched you back and then Kelly said well I think that I will be fine and then Mike grab and push down Kelly and he ran to the ladder and Mark and Leo were left behind with Kelly and then she said did he leaves bullets to shoot them? Then Leo checks the gun and said it is empty and we will be dead. About one hour later, they heard that Mike was screaming and being torn into pieces and Kelly said I guess we are safe if we when with Mike we probably end up dead, so he did something right! But we are still trap and we don't have a place to runs.

Well I think we should go to the bottom of the mall and get to the car and get the hell out of here.

Hope that your right, Kelly! I think I am, but I hope that we get way! So we need to do it now and later will be too late, yes go get your stuff and let start moving before they reach the top and we are goner, so you smart Kelly, but I do have that survive in me and I don't give up and I just don't want to died here! Let go now!! So we will follow you Kelly we are behind you, good. Later that night they climb the ladder and they saw the zombies and Kelly said hurried and they didn't stops on the lower level and just kept on going. Then Kelly started to scream and they got my leg, help me Mark and Leo, I don't wants to be goner, and then Mark climb down and hit the zombie but the zombies grab Mark, and meanwhile Leo and Kelly escape and Kelly said we need to help Mark, well he is probably dead all ready! No, I am not leaving him, so ahead I am leaving!

Kelly said bye to Leo and at that moment Leo got caught with zombies surrounded him and he called out for Help! Kelly do you hear me!!!

But Kelly didn't comes and he was about to get slaughter by the zombies and Kelly started to shoot the zombies and grab Leo and Mark and they ran into the bar and locked the door. They will break in and we will die tonight! I don't wants to hear that Leo, and Mark was barely alive and he loss a lot of blood and he got infection and he will turned into a zombie, so how do you know that's? I saw it happened before and we need to shoot him in the head, well he is my friend and I will shoot him.

Then Kelly said don't wait just shoot him, he is still not turning and then I said your going wait until he does and killed us? No!

He might not change into those undead and you only want to kill, kills!

I want to survive this nightmare don't you?

Yes I do shoot him now, and then he felt his pulse and it was gone and then a second later, he woke up and became a zombie, shot him in the head and he was dead.

Now Kelly and Leo were the only one left in bar and zombies were coming toward the bar and they were smelling us and I knew that we had to move fast to be dead meat for the zombies.

Next Day, Zombies VS Human

Kelly said to Leo now what? I don't know exactly but we need to get out of here and gets to that car and drive away from here and that was the plan that Mike and Mark had but I didn't listens to them and now they are dead and I blame myself for this and Kelly said it is my fault I should not comes, and this tragedy and you loss your friends, and I feel awful, but Kelly it is not your fault, but the one that may that chemical spill.

Turn the dead into zombies, I know you are talking about the government for this fatso, yes and I they need to be alert what going on!

Are you saying that you will call up the government and tell them, they probably known what happening, and then they heard planes flying over there head and Kelly said yes, they will save us! How do you know they probably will kill us? No I don't wants to hears that Kelly.

I been through many tragedy in my life and I don't wants to lose my life and I do wants to survive this and tells others.

I think that we are the only one alive, said Kelly! Leo said no there must be more, and about a minute later, they heard a truck and some shooting and then it stops and knock at the door and said let us in.

Kelly was about to open the door, and Leo said don't open the I door, it might be Zombies, how could it be, well they are more smarter and they are much faster, well we need to find out they need our help, and he called out and said let me in and I am Jon. Are you one a zombie? No I am human and I am not going to get killed and Kelly open the door and he walks and said close it quickly, and about one minute later they were at the door at the bar, and we need to get back on my truck and leave this place now. So where are we going?

22

I don't know but we will get slaughter here. Fine I am ready.

So what is the plan? Well the plan is too shoot the zombies and make sure that they are dead, of course they are the undead but they really need to shot in the head, so about the vampires/ zombies those are more difficulty one to killed, so why? Well one place you need to stake and shoot in the head, oh I sees! I think that we will be able to do that's!

Yes, but you really didn't says what exactly going to do when there are like thousand of them coming closer to us… so runs and fight back I am trying and they are gained up on me and hurry Leo, I don't wants to died today! You won't so how do you known? I don't know…I see the truck so you have the key to start up the truck and we can leaves this place, so where we go it will be the same… don't says that's Leo.

Kelly got to the truck and got inside and she was looking for Leo and Mark to comes, and about a minute later she saw them and also the zombies, and I called out and said hurried they are getting closer and Mark fell to the ground and Leo said I have too gets him and I said watched out that zombies is about a inch away from you.

Mark got up and Leo started to runs and runs and they got to the truck and Leo said I drop the keys and I need to go back, and I said no!

If I don't go back we will be stuck here and we will end up dead, and about one second later, Leo crawled on the ground and spread his clothes that smell like the dead and crawled half way and then he grab the keys and turned around and there was a zombies but didn't touch him and then he crawled very slowly and he reach the truck and pull off the smelling shirt and got inside started up and they drove away.

Then Kelly said well, you really risk your life for us and hope that we can do the same, and he said we needed to gets way and I had too do it.

Then Kelly fell asleep and Mark and Leo said so where are we going? I don't know but I know that we need to leave the New York and head south to Florida? Yes is that a good ideas, at this point I believe yes.

I don't think that Kelly will be happy with our decision and I think it is the right one. I hope so Leo, so we will have to fight with the zombies and we will have to win! That true, and I cannot disagree with you.

About two hour later Kelly woke up and said how long did I sleep?

Two hours, wow, why didn't you wake me? Well you were sleeping peaceful, but still you should have woke me up and so where are headed? (Florida) what are frigging out of your mind, what are you saying? There are many zombies there and we are going to gets killed and you need to turn the car around and headed to Texas. So what different in Texas, you didn't hear the broadcast that Texas is the safe house from Zombies, and they called it safe heaven, yes!

Leo said to Mark, I think that I when the wrong ways and so I will turn the truck around and head to Texas,, and then Kelly put on the radio and there was a "special News" said the country is invaded by the undead and there is mayhem in the street.

Now what? I don't know what to do? We are really not safe.

Ok! They are headed toward us and they getting close and they are near the car, no, yes. They are going to grabbing me, and then they pull her back.

Then Leo took the shoot it in the head, and I have three bullets left.

What are going here? I don't know but we cannot stay here your right!

They got out of car and walking in the path, one zombie coming toward Kelly, then Leo knocks it down. Kelly ran toward LEO...

He grabs her and they kissed, Mark said not now!!! We need to wait until went we are safe and Kelly, fine and they kissed again! Then zombies came from nowhere.

Runs, said Kelly, to Mark, and Leo, I will catch up and we will be fine.

When they got to the four corner, and they seen a red barn and they would about to approach the farm, the farmer comes out shooting them and zombies are coming near. Mark said duck down and crawled on the ground, and they snuck behind the farmer, and Leo hit the farmer and fell to the ground and Mark grab the gun...

ZOMBIES COMING TO THE FARM!

The farmer said "let me go" I will not harm you; well you tried to killed us.

No, I refuse, I don't trust you, so where are the rest of bullets, I don't have anymore, and we will search your house. But don't hurt my daughter SARAH, we won't, promise and SARAH came out of house, daddy, where are you? Then Leo said I thought she was a little girl, but she is a beautiful woman with light skin and slim body with a pretty smile and gorgeous long blonde hair, and blue eyes, and wearing those short shorts and low cut blouse. Then Leo called out and said there is a zombie in back, and she slip and about to be bitten and Leo ran out to her grab into the barn and close the door and said why did you tied up my dad, he was going to shoot us, because he thought we were zombies but we are not!!!

Listens" let my dad go"! No he wanted to shoot us and I don't trust you and I just wants my dad to be frees, and Leo said ok! Promise not to shoot us? He nodded his head and they untied him and at that moment a zombie broke in and he pick up the rifle and shoot the zombie in the head.

Then Leo asked Sarah, are you seeing anyone? And Kelly got angry and was about to walk out of the barn and Mark stops her, and Kelly was about to walks into Zombies, and suddenly they close the door and added more wood and make it secure. It will keep the zombies out for a while but we need to leaves soon! I will not leave my dad and he refuse to go and I am staying with him. You both must comes with us and you cannot stay here, we are not going, and then it was a boom and they broke in and they were coming toward them and they ran out of the barn and they were surrounded by the zombies, then Sarah ran out and use a stick over the

25

head and a few zombies fell down dead, Leo, and Mark, Kelly, come on and now it is time, to runs! Then Sarah said that my dad is hurt, no! He was hurt, he had been bitten, he will become a zombie, and no I will get that poison infection out his body, your going, to kill him.

No, I just to want says he will be dead, no he will not be.

Then she pull out a gun and pointed toward them, Kelly, Mark, Leo, and don't, move, Sarah what are you doing? I need to save him, so you get the knife. No I am not I am not touching him, I am not getting infection.

Leo said we going so if shoot us go head you will be defeat by the zombies, I don't care. You should, let us go!

So Sarah said go I am not keeping you so leave get ambush, and Sarah opened the door, then a zombies grab by her arm and pull her and she got bitten and about ten zombies started to eat her up and it was body parts and blood splatter, and then the farmer woke up has a zombie.

Leo shoots him the head, and he dead. Then more zombies enter barn, Leo is trap and Kelly and Mark, said we will save you man!

Don't leaves me,! We won't leave and then he got grab and torn apart.

No, no, no, he is dead, now we are still trap but we might end up dead don't says that Kelly, we are going make out alive and we couldn't help him. But we need to move now, fine.

Then the storm came thunder and lighting, hit the barn and it started a fire. Kelly ran out and Mark said what are you doing?

Are you bait? You're planning to get killed so you better move, so you really care what happened to me? No! So I will stand here and I will not died take my word. Fine! So I will just let you stand there and I will. Get to the truck and drive way? No you need to wait for me and don't leave me behind, no I wont! Comes I cannot wait to be somewhere safe and then we will not fight with the zombies and but they will be around until the government killed them if they are able killed them and duplicate, and I know but let worry, but we just can stand around and get away from the farm and I don't know where to go and I don't where we will be safe but I know we just cannot stay here and we need to move now.

Yes you are right! I know that I am but I need you too be quiet and then I need which ways to go through the woods but or the dirt road and toward the town with the most popularity and that is not a good idea about that we might end up end and or becoming zombies, but please don't let it happen to me!

I am scare Mark, and Kelly said I am frighten and I think that we might end up dead don't says that Kelly.

Just walks and follow the ways I am going and we will be safe.

Are you sure? Yes I am so I think getting away from the farm to the city and our chances might be better.

Not sure!

So do you wants to stay here and sees how many are coming closer.

I know! It is a nightmare that will not end and we need to not to be caught or bitten, and then Kelly called out Mark, did you sees the sign, that this area is restricted, and will be shot at sight.

Then Kelly said we are not going there! No we are not, you are right!

Looks Mark, and those zombies are behind the gates and we near to go the different direction and headed south of here.

Ok!

Kelly was holding his hand and walks through the path and turned right!

"Ambush"

Kelly and Mark were headed south and then they when cross the bridge the and they saw a town and Kelly said why don't we go there!

Ok , and Kelly and Mark when over the bridge and then Kelly when into the grocery store and Mark said are you sure that you wants to go inside and Kelly said yes I do! But you can tell me when we need to runs if we run into zombies, I think this place is no-zone zombies.

I am glad that we can rest and pick up some foods and find a hotel and then we can just go into the suite and then we can rest and eat our foods.

They enter the hotel and which floor should we take well the lower floor but not that safe that true and the higher floor for escape and it is a bit risking that true and so which floor I think the 11 floor will do but it is still high and do you have a plan to escape no I don't! Says if we are not alone, we are fine for the night and we will leave in the morning.

Why are you so confident? Well, I believe that we should be positive and so I am...

Then Mark said are we going to sleep in the same bed? No we are not!

I am just asking and so Kelly took the bed near the window and said goodnight Mark, and then Mark came over to her and tried to kiss her.

Kelly slapped his face and pushes him off the floor and then Kelly said did you hear that'? What I don't understand what your saying!

I think someone is downstairs, and so there are more peoples and not zombies around, I hope so.

Mark said I will check it out and I will be back in five minutes and then Kelly said I am not staying alone here and I am coming with you.

Fine! Comes Kelly we will just go by the stairs and then just peek inside and sees if they are not zombies, but then we will not let them sees us.

But why not they must want to steal from us and we will be hungry and we wills died. Now, you are really scaring and I don't like what you are saying Mark.

They got on the bottom floor and they were about to sees that they were and it was like the "zombies" had followed them there!

Are they zombies? Yes they are and they are very hungry and they want brains.

Comes on they cannot smell us, because we are alive and they will wants our brains. Yes I know and I don't have a gun or bullets to shoot them.

You lost the gun and bullets, you ass. How could you and our lives.

Don't be such a bitch and you know what our odd are and you know that the zombies might gets us, no I think to make it alive.

You must be living in a fantasy world, no I am not. But hurried we need to barriers us in the room and make sure that we are safe Mark.

But they still could come up and break the doors and reach our room and eat us up.

They ran alls the ways up stairs and locked the door and kept it close and then they heard a big bang and the other side of the walls collapse on Mark, and Kelly tried to wake him up.

About a minute later, two zombies were into the room and approach them and Kelly said what now? Just don't stand there!

Then they would go closer and closer and Mark said they are going to get us and don't let them, I will try not too. But they were trap and they were out of bullets and no weapons and they were about to bite Kelly, and someone came into the building and her name was Karen and Rick and called out and said comes on we can leave now! Are you sure? Yes and they walks into thousand zombies and Kelly said you trick us. No but they needed foods and so we let you be ambush and be dead meat for zombies, but why I don't understand you don't even know me, and you are like my enemy, but I am a friend of the zombies. That why you put us into this situation, yes! Then Kelly started to beat up Karen and Rick and Jim and Kelly had a battle and at that moment.

Rick fell between the five zombies and then Karen called out I will save you, so your plan backfire... no, but I am not going let Rick get killed.

Then Mark and Karen and Kelly somehow to get Rick out of zone of the zombies and he was safe and then they when inside and close the door and make sure that they were safe, but Kelly and Mark didn't trust Karen and Rick, and then the ran came down and then the door open and Kelly said they are coming in here! No, yes!

Do you have a gun? No, and we are dead meat, and I thought they were your friends, but they still wants my brains too. Oh!

I guess the hunted are being hunting by the zombies, and we still might make it alive from here, are sure, no! Now I am scare and I don't wants to be here, but Rick bought us here and now, I feel trap.

Then Kelly said we will find a way out and we will get way and why are you so calm. Well I when through a lot here.

I know what you mean, and then we will get to the black car and drive ways and not looking back, well someone has to be bait and then we will be escape, and Rick said I will volunteer for this task. Are really sure? Yes! Can we trust you? I am doing it and risking my life and you might survive the ordeal and we will be traveling together.

That true but it will not affect my thinking of you. Fine! Give me five minutes and you and Karen and Kelly runs to the car and start it up and I should be there in five minutes myself.

Ok! First Rick step out and making noises and the zombies would getting close to him and Kelly and Karen and Mark ran to the car, and Karen looked for Rick and the plan was to drive up and pickup Rick.

Rick standing and about to be bitten by five zombies and then the car drove up and pick him out and Mark hits a few zombies and put on the gas and drove away very quickly and didn't looked back.

Well I am still fine and in one piece and not bitten and it was a great job, Mark, at that moment I thought you were leave me here! Well I did think about it and your girlfriend Karen were not be happy with me, that true, she were stop the car and threw you out and you were be dead.

When you look at Karen she has dark black hair and short and have a piercing on her body and leather jacket and leather pants and shirt and a cap. About five feet and 7 inch tall and back languages, then they stop and Mark said why you told me to stop and Karen and Rick said we should make love in the woods, and Kelly said are you both will put his danger, why can we just keeps going and then went we are safer, no I am horny for him, well you too just can sit here! Then Karen said Rick makes sure that you take the keys from the car and we don't want them to leave. We need to go now before we are trap and be bitten and become a zombies or even dead.

But the car will not start I think it is out of gas and that great! We are unable to be safe but end of being dead, I did plan it this ways!

I didn't neither, then Kelly said stop fighting and think of a plan to be safe from here, we are but not working, comes I been in worst situation and I am still alive good for you and I hate being here.

So what can we do? Well survive and try to make it too Atlantic City and maybe we will be safe there! Ok!

Is that a good idea? I don't know but we should try but we are still in New York and we have a long ways to gets there and we need to get there I think there are no zombies there! Ok let go and but we need to find a car with gas and get the hell out of here immediately and I mean now., do you understand yes I do so let go, I am following you and so are they.

"Do you think that we will make it"? I hope so we cannot died here and b what the government, are saying that it is the government fault yes if the spill and it when into the water and the foods that we eat and it is not a good things and we need to be careful what we drink and eat because is spread very quickly and then you died and you become a zombies.

So we shouldn't drink the bottle water or the water from the faucet?

Do we know what good and what bad, no we don't know but it is a risk that we need to takes no thanks! But I see a car ahead and I will go ahead and sees if it work but do a distract that I wont be bitten about us.

When I started the car I will drive toward you and Karen and we will leave here, so can we trust you? Comes on we did deal with the zombies and I didn't leaves you girls behind so, no I will not abandon you.

So he started to walks a mile and he saw the red Chevy car and when toward it and was about to step inside but the zombies caught him but Kelly ran up with a stick and hit the zombie and Karen follow her and they alls when inside the car and drove away.

Now we are on our ways and i hope that we have enough gas to reach Atlantic City New Jersey, great!

Location New Jersey

They were driving for hours and hours and then they stop at the New Jersey gas station but it was abandon and no one in sight and then Kelly said I have a bad a feeling about this place why? No one is around and it seems like there is no one alive.

I think that you are just thinking that the zombies are everywhere so I will go to the restroom and I will be back in five minutes, ok!

Meanwhile Kelly said to Mark, think that she is all right! I believe that she will be back soon and then we can leave and head to Atlantic City, and that is great! Yep! Here she comes, looks how she is walking and she is not alone, looks zombies are following her. That not good!

Looked at her face no she is one of them. No she is not but they will catch her so drive up to her now, you must be kidding, no I am not! Go to her and called out to her and tell her that don't stand, there, because they will shred her into pieces and she will be dead.

They drove up to her and then they notice that she was a zombies and he speed way and when toward the highway and said we are not making no more stops unless we need too. Fine!

Once again I feel that I loss a friend but I didn't know her that well but still the zombies are winning and hope that we survive this ordeal of mayhem and hell that we are going through.

Don't worry Kelly we will find a way and we will not become zombies so how do you know? I don't know but one thing I am not going to change, and I will think how to make it and so will you.

They were about 250 miles away from Atlantic city, New Jersey, and are you sure that zombies will not comes out of the water of Atlantic City and be a whole bunch of zombies on the broad walks of Atlantic City, I don't know what kind of situation we will have to deal with but we will be ready.

But I do like how you think and most of alls not to separate but stick together, yes I do understand, so listen what I says to you, most of the times, sometime you can be wrong, that true.

They were city limit of Atlantic City and I cannot wait to gets there and I know that I need to called home and sees if my family fine.

So where do they lives in Orlando Florida, and I think that they are safe.

Hope that they are; now they reach the city and it was quiet and no one on the street and Kelly said, where are alls the peoples? I don't know maybe inside playing the slots, I hope so, and then the storm came in and Mark said I will park in the garage, on the lower level.

Will we be able to escape if we needed too I believe that we will.

So he park the car and they got out of the car and got inside the elevator and when to the upper floor to the casino and they heard music and peoples screaming and jumping up and down, and Kelly said seem like it normal and we should be fine, and you are right!

The moment that they step inside the casino they knew that they were safe, so then they when downstairs and looked around and then they heard a banged and then they saws "Zombies coming toward them. So Kelly immediately step inside the elevator and when back to the car and so they were also in the garage, well Mark we are in trouble.

But how they are coming and we cannot gets out of here if we do we will be lucky what are you saying we are stuck in the zombies world.

I am not going to give up and I am going to fight it, do you hears me Karen and Mark? Yes we do but we better move quick to survive this ordeal and maybe we will have a tiny chance, I like what you are saying but we just cannot just stand around here and get bitten and turned into those zombies, ok let started running from here and no stopping do you understand, we are exhaust, I know but you don't wants to be dead meat, no I don't said Karen and Mark so move on. But don't gets caught., sure, I won't and you neither said Kelly.

I have loss a lot of my friends because of this and I do want to make it alive and hope some of my family are not zombies, but I will deal with that if I have too and right I just wants to stay alive. Me too, said Karen and Mark, ok we are ready to leaves this dead zone, so am I!

About two hour later, they were near Atlantic City and that is in New Jersey, and Karen said is this a good idea to go to a casino?

You know that the other casino are infection and I hope this one is safe and without zombies, and well it clear so far, so I think that the bally grand might be the safe house for now, so you are making decision about our lives and we don't have to says anything about it, no you don't, our lives might be cut short and you are taking control so we would like to decided what we wants to stays or leaves this place, ok!

About two hour later,, the rain and thunder storms came through and it was really rainy hard and Mark said that is not a good signs. What do you means, I think that we will be surrounded by the zombies when we step out, and how do you know that's! It happened in Seattle and it happened quickly, you don't says and what else?

We need to secure this place but we cannot because it is too big.

I know that Mark, and it is very dangerous and risking to stay here, and then Mark looked out and said they are coming out of the water, no, yes they are Kelly, there are thousand coming toward the broad walks and they will comes inside and catch us, we need to gets to the garage and leave this place immediately, do you understand Kelly, I do know what you mean? So let go now before they reach us so where do we go to Pennsylvania, ok! They alls got inside the elevator and when to the garage and then they were going toward the car and then they came. And Mark said I told you so what will happen and it did.

Ok I should have listened to you, so let go now.

They alls got inside the car and the car were not started up and then it did they drove off and speeding out of the garage into the highway and now they saw them in the road out of Atlantic City and Mark said that is not good, I know we stay here too long and now our lives are in danger and we will become zombies, don't says that Mark said Karen.

'Do you see them? No I think they are gone... but we need to be on our guard when we gets to Pennsylvania, and I think there are no zombies there so how do you know that's ? I am just thinking loud, and ok!

So, how many miles to gets the? I don't know but we are very close, that is good but the zombies are following us. That is not good said Kelly.

About twenty minutes later, they were in Pennsylvania, and they were relief and felt safe and they went to comfort motel and check in and the man said how many rooms? They said three, and he looked and said I only have one, so do you wants to take it? They shook there head and said yes we will take it and the man said don't go out at night. Ok! But they didn't understand what he was saying that moment.

Now it was getting dark and Karen said I need to take a smoke and I will be right out of the door and Kelly said didn't you hears what the man said? Yes I did, but I will be fine. I believe that you should stay inside.

No, I am going out and getting some fresh air, ok so ahead I am not stopping you, fine and I don't want to be order around by anyone, do you understand? Fine! The minute that she step out, and she started to looked and then they approach her and said let me in now, what wrong, zombies, what? Gets inside right now! Karen step inside and then they started to banged the door and window and we need to block and locked it and be secure because they will be able be safe so the check in ,man knew the situation and he didn't tells us, I know but he did warns us.

You right and we should be quiet and we don't even have a weapon to shoot, what will do we? I don't know but what will happen to us.

But I will not died today or tomorrow, I will not let be killed. I will fight to the end and I will not be caught by the undead to you understand Karen and Mark. I when through a lot and I am not giving up, and I won't they took the chair and close the door and window and we will be safe tonight.

Are you sure we will be safe? Yes! Ands we will leave, ok!

Fine and better move, now...

I am ready so am I. ok so let go now... I am ready to go yes but hurried.

I am in back of you and but don't leave me and I won't and we will be together, yes. We will.

Later that night they went to the car and drove off and said so where should we go now? I don't know...

But I am starving and I need something to eat but if we stop we will get eaten up by the zombies, no! I will be careful.

Karen step inside the diner and it seem fine.. then they alls when inside and sat in the booth and then no one came and Karen got up.

Dead Zone

It is so silent and no one is around and I don't like this and I am scared that someone will pop up and it will be a zombies and what then?

We will become to be undead and we will wants to eat brains, and I am not a meat lover, I am vegetable person, so you will be different.

No, I wants to stay alive and not be dead and I want to have love and happier, to Mark said Kelly.

Do you understand sure I do and I want the same but I never found my true love, well you know that time is running out and we are in a bad place at this moment, yes but we will not give up said Mark?

But we are not getting stronger but weaker and we might lose the war and I will not do that.

Then Mark said there is no activity here and I think that there are no zombies up this location.

So far you right and we need to be sure and yes we need to looks around and make sure that we will not gets any surprises, yes we do!

But now we need someone a watched and two of you will sleep and if something happened and we need to leave right oh ways we will, yes.

Karen and Kelly, when to sleep in the sleeping bag and they shut the door with some woods and the windows and then Mark drank a lot of coffee and then he fell asleep and about ten minutes,

Ten minutes later they were coming into the room and no one heard a sound until, I somehow heard some noise that I thought it was outside but it was right next to me and I didn't know how to move and says something to my friends that we just got invades by the zombies.

But somehow I manage to get up very slowly and walks toward Karen and touch her shoulder and whisper,, they are inside the room.

We need to reach Mark and wake him up and go around, the zombies and we will get out of the room, but be quiet and walks toward the door and don't make the sound and they do smell us.

But then Karen said, ok! But I forgot my purse and I need to takes it and my cell phone and we need to called someone, but to the police maybe the military, you mean the army or the marines? Yes!

Make sure that you don't slam the door I won't! that moment she said it so how the door slams and they started to comes out of the motel and started to go after us. I didn't know but I ran quick to the car and they asked me what wrong and I said I just forgot and I slams the door and now they will eat our brains, don't worry I will started up the car and we will leave this place and go to Orlando Florida and go to World Dinsey, that sound nice, I guess if we won't runs into zombies.

Not sure but now they are leaving Pennsylvania, great! Well we runs into Amish Zombies I don't know, hope not.

Meanwhile Karen lies down in the backseat and fell asleep and they were driving and then they hit the rock and then Karen got up and said what happened well he ran into a rock and but no damage to the car,, why don't you watched how your driving, well, well, smarty pants, I did not have sleep for 24 hours and you had six hours and you are bossy me around so why don't you started driving and gets us out of here.

Fine but you never asked I will drive and you can sleep and I will run down the zombies if I have too, now you sound that you are just a being just a smart ass and so be quiet and I am trying to drive out of here, and get to civilization and not being surrounded by zombies.

Ok! So do I go on 95 and headed toward Florida? Yes that is the plan so do we have enough gas to get there? I think so but I don't want to be stranded and without gas do you understand? Totally!

Are sure that we are going south on 95 yes and no turning back, I do understand where ever it lead us., yes and we have no choice to turned back. That is true but I don't want to be mistaken, fine.

Then Kelly remark are you lover, yes once we were but not anymore. So what happen because he wanted to boss me around and I refuse and we decided to become friends and then this disaster happen and we stay together, oh I sees! So I can date him and you won't mind at alls.

But I didn't says that I still love him and I do care for him so you can eat your cake and have him too that is unfair.

I think that he is very attractive and I do want him because my boyfriend got eaten by the zombies, well his name was Mike, and then it was Leo.

So you had a lot of boyfriends no but a lot of sex partner, I don't want to hears this and Mark said I do. I want to have sex before I died.

Karen said well I will have it with you, well I had you and I want with someone new. But right now just focus on the road and get us out of here.

I will don't worry and we will be there in two days and we will be safe.

Don't say something that you are not sure of.

Comes on I am getting tired once again and we need to rest somewhere and I don't know if we are going to reach Florida.

Your going the wrong ways, I don't think so said Mark, and don't refuse me and I need to go alls the ways on 95 and we will be there.

Don't listen to her, said Karen, she does not know what she is saying and I think that she is infection and we should dump her out of the car now.

Are you crazy and I am not infection she might be, and then Mark stop the car and said let me looks at your arm, Karen?

No, don't listen to that bitch, and then Kelly said looks into her eyes and you will tell if she is infection, so you smart Kelly. I went through a lot and I know how the symptoms are and how it runs it course.

Yes and she is acting a bit strange, thanks! Next you will be saying that I will turn into a zombies yes and you will tried too eat our brains.

No, I will not turn into the zombies, but they are coming toward us.

Zombies are coming

I sees them and I feel that I am changing and I don't know but probably I did gets bit by that zombies at the motel and now I will be one so shoot me I don't want to eat your brain, Mark. I don't even have a gun to shoot you, just hit my head and put into my brain, and I will immediately died.

They are not too far from us so we better leaves and just tell Karen to gets out of the car because I am afraid that she might bite me first and then you will have too killed both.

So Kelly push out Karen out of the car and Mark said is you out of your mind? No but I am trying to save us. No I am not leaving my friend here, she is coming with us do you understand? Yes.

But she might bite us and she will turn into in few minutes and we need to killed her now and not later do you understand? Yes but just leaves I don't think so, we need to take her to the hospital and they cannot help her if there is a hospital, probably the zombies are in control we don't know that Mark, we don't but we need to find out and get our lives in danger and I don't think so said Mark. I think that we should take her now, I thought you were joking, but you are serious about doing that's? Yes, if you were the one we should leave you? No! But looked at her, I am she is changing in front of us and you still wants to save her, and I don't get it, Kelly, I think that you want a death wish, no I don't I just want to make it alive, well what you are trying to do with Karen, you probably will be a goner.

Stop saying that's! ok I will and so let go now!!!

It should be about half hour to get to the hospital and then she will get better so how do you know that's? I think she will. Unless she died and turn into a zombies and you will be her first meal, stop saying that Mark, but it is true, about ten minute away they were there and Kelly said stop the car and we will bring her in, ok! But Mark was a bit hesitates about doing that because he knew that the hospital is where the zombies are.

But he kept quiet and Kelly called out and no one came to them and they place Karen on the bed and Kelly walks around and looked and said no one here, I think that we should leave, and Mark said I told you this was a mistake, I know I should have listen to you but I was wrong and Mark said leave her on the bed, and Kelly said no, she is coming with us, and about a minute later, Kelly felt her pulse and there was nothing and Kelly said I think she will become a zombies so shoot her in the head, but I don't have a weapon. Just hit she in back of her head hard and she will die for really.

But I cannot do it, so Mark when up to her and mash her head and now we can go, and ok I am ready, they were about to step out of there and there were zombies standing out there and now what?

Ok! Take some of the clothes from Karen and let them think that we are dead and we will be able to go and they will not follow us, unless they are advance Zombies, I think they are and I don't like this scenario. I don't neither but we have no choice, I know, I will disaster them and you go to the car and we will be fine, I am not leaving you to defend for yourself.

So do you want to be stuck here? No!

About five minute later, Mark somehow manage to get to the car and Meanwhile that Kelly was trying to get to Mark, and then he drove up with the car and I ran to the car and one zombie try to grab my hand and I pull away and I was safe inside the car and we drove away and said we need to get back on the highway and not be in the dark and we need to find a place to sleep do you understand but we are going south and we will get to west palm and we will stay there for few days, until I figure out a plan to be safe and not be attack by the zombies, yes.

I still sees them coming toward us and I think that will follow us, hope that you are wrong about that. No, some are smarter and they remember how they were and I also heard that they know how to drive a car and that is not true, said Mark, it is ridicule and you really make a mess because of Karen, I was trying to help her, so you risks ours lives for her.

Some barking at me, and listens you need to know that there is a place that they have cured for infection, I don't believe what you are saying too me, stop talking I need silent to think, all right!

Later that night Mark somehow he find the highway and left Orlando and went toward West Palm beach and stop for gas and Kelly was fast asleep in the car and Mark when into the restroom and stay for while and about five minutes later, he came out and he was surrounded by the zombies, and in the car, Kelly was sleeping and he was yelling and screaming and she didn't hear him, but suddenly she woke up very quick and saw the zombies were near the car and Mark was trap. And now Kelly had to think what to do and save Mark, so she looked in the backseat of the car and she find a pistol and check for bullets and then she came out of car and started to shoot them in the head and she called out to Mark to run out and he said, are you crazy and she said do you wants to be dead meat, and he said no I don't so just runs and don't gets caught, easy said then done said Mark, I am going to be "Dead meat" for the zombies, and then she said what possession to leave me here alone and you just looking around and you knew that there were zombies around and more and more are coming!!!

But Kelly and Mark, make it too the car and drove off with the gas pump in the car and it almost blew up and she said are crazy we could been dead if the gas pump blew up but we are not and we are safe away from the zombies that true, and I don't how long our luck will last.

Mark said we have about two miles to get there and I think that we will make it but why you choose West palm beach, well it thought it were be no zombies around and will be safe well we are taking chances to survive this nightmare, yes we are so be quiet.

They were getting closer and closer toward west palm beach and suddenly the car stops and Kelly looked at him and they started to kiss and kiss and then they make love all night long and then Mark said if this is our last night together I wants to be with you and Kelly smiles and said,, I wants the same and I don't wants to let you go and then Mark said, I need to stretch my feet, and Kelly said I wants to do the same, well let me check it out first if it is safe and so he looked around and seems like it will be fine. That day Mark and Kelly walks on the beach and they make love and lies on the sand and near the water, and about a minute later, Kelly said did you hears that sound, it must be the ocean and I hope that you are right.

The sun was going in and it was getting dark and Kelly said I think that we should go back to the car, and he said I am conformable here, so Kelly left him and said I will meet you at the car.

Kelly walks toward the car and change her clothes and looked around and seem everything was normal, and then Kelly saw something in the bush, and she called out to Mark and said comes to me, I miss you very much. I will be there in five minutes, but hurried, said Kelly, so what going on, please comes I will feel better, when you are with me.

So he pick up his stuff and then looked into the Atlantic ocean and he saw the zombies and he ran to the car and he almost slip on the sand but he came to the car and said we need to leave now.

What wrong Mark? Zombies are coming and we need to go now, I don't believe you, looks at the ocean, ok I don't sees anything, are you blind?

No! Once again, Kelly looked out and said, ok I sees them, now we need to go and I am glad that you believe me and they both got inside the car and they drove off, and there were over thousand of them.

Mark drove like a mad man and Kelly said I don't want to end up in accident and I just want to be safe and I think that we should go to the airport and take a plane to Los Angeles, are you losing your mind?

No, I am not maybe the plane are flying out of here from the zombies coast of Florida, ok we will go to the west palm beach airport and buy a ticket back to the west coast, but it does crazy, I knows it does but I do want to get back there, but that is like zombie land, maybe not.

About five miles south to airport and I don't know why I am listening you.

But I will even though it sound crazy and I am still doing it.

I am tired of driving and it is your turn, fine I will take over.

About two minute later, they reach the airport and Mark said looks.

What am I looking at? Looks at alls these peoples at the airport and they are board planes out of here.

So we need to buy a tickets non stop to LA and I will go to the rest room and clean up and so Mark when up to the counter and bought a tickets and on Atlantic west and about ten minutes later they board the plane.

Mark and Kelly sat next the window and Kelly was relax and Mark was not.

Non- stop flight to LA

Mark looks at Kelly and said maybe we should get off this flight I have a bad feeling and he said I don't wants to be here.

Kelly said there are no zombies on the flight and about five hours from now we will be home, and one passenger, and Mark said looked at him,, so he got some burned, but he is no zombies, how do you know.

We will be fine. Soon has the plane goes up we can end up being dead meat, I am not staying, and Kelly said, you are overtired and overreaction about this flight, are scare to fly no I just don't wants to died, if you stay here you will, I don't to listen too, you were wrong about the hospital and you could be wrong about this flight. Are you sure that we will be fine? Yes we are and don't worry about it, but I do have a bad feeling about this flight and I just relax before you know it we will be home and everyone will be fine, I know what your saying but we are still invaded by the zombies and this world will not be the same, when the zombies gone!

Here comes the flight attended and said do you something to eat or drink and but the plane didn't go up yet but still at the gate and Mark and I said no, and then some more passengers came on and it was ten more persons but they really looks different, and Mark said they look like Zombies, no way, looked at them, you are right and the door was close on the plane, so says a lot of prays and we will be eaten by the zombies, now we can says we do have a problem.

Just sit and be quiet and we will be fine and don't make any move, ok I will sit like bait and no suddenly move, ok! But they are looking at us and the other passenger, yes! One of the passengers got up and walks by us and started to smell us and at that moment, I thought I was a goner, and then she spoke and said what kind of perfume you are wearing.

Chanel 5 and you smell nice and then said to me, we are not how we looks but we are just being in disguise, and try not to get bitten by the zombies and this is like a five hour flight and we are on our guard and ok!

The third passenger was about to get up but sat down and then the plane was on the runaway and soon the plane will be in the sky.

At this moment I started to have a panic attack and I didn't know what to do but I just couldn't sit but I needed to move.

But Mark said just sit down and be quiet we don't need the attention.

Ok, and Kelly I think that your right and I think we should have driven to LA but huh! We are going up in the air and now we are stuck here and we have nothing to fight with and we could end up dead, and I will not blame you, and then the captain spoke and said everyone keep your seatbelt on and we will have a little turbine in shaking and then suddenly the plane was like nose dive and now Mark and Kelly hold hands and now what are we going to died now? No!

About one minute later the plane was in the attitudes and it level up and they were headed to LA, and Kelly was looking out of the window and praying alls the ways there!

Then the storm came and the plane shaking up and down.

About two hours later, Mark and Kelly fell asleep and then the chaos happen and they slept through the whole thing, and about one hour later and they were near the LAX airport and Kelly looks around and the plane was going lower and lower reaching the destination and Kelly said where are the rest of the passenger, and Kelly said soon has the plane land, we should just go off and runs very quickly and open the door.

Mark got up and he saw bodies parts and blood on the plane and then about a minute before the plane to land, two zombies were coming toward him, but they didn't touch him, because he had the smell, and Kelly said, they didn't touch you, and then they landed in LAX and the plane when to the gate and the park the plane and the door of the plane open and now they walks out and Kelly and Mark said, looks it seem like we will be fine, at that moment the Zombies were in the gates and now what? So we just walks by them and be just like them.

Hope that your right? So they walks very slowly when outside and took a park car and drove away from the airport, I think that we did wrong, by taking someone car and Mark said they will not miss the car and how do you know I don't! About one hour later they when to CBS near the farmer market and I wants to know if I can buy coffee and some breakfast, well you like taking risk, well I am home and I wants to be sure that everything is fine. Of course, and they both walks in the parking a lot and then there are thousand of zombies here, and we will be killed for sure. Don't says that Kelly, I won't but it could be true, bit your tongue, no!

No they see us runs, to the car and let headed out of here.

So where should drive to San Vicente, and we will head toward Disneyland and we should be fine. Once again you are telling me what to do! About one hour later they arrival and they knew that they might be safe for a while but they know that they couldn't stay long.

Now what I though we were going to be safe in LA but the infection started here and it will end here, what you saying the chemical spill happened here next too the ocean and we will be infection by them and we will become them, don't says that Mark, just trust me.

We need to go to the chemical plants and looked for the cure and save the world,. It might be too late… my family is here in the Westwood; well they are probably the dead.

No, no, no, I will not died today or tomorrow I will fight with my last breathe that I take, sure. I am not giving up and so we need to fight and win the war, that is true and I will not disagree.

So they got inside the car and knock down a few zombies on the ways and then them when on the freeway and headed to "Westwood".

"Westwood Zombies"

Are you sure that we are going the right ways? Yes!

We are in Westwood and there are a thousand of zombies and has bad has at the airport and what are we going to do so the plan is to go to my house and then gets my parents out and take them with us, but they might be zombies alls ready said Kelly and I really don't have the have the strength to fight or walks, but you need to be strong Mark and if you are not we are going to lose our lives, that is true and I don't wants to be dead meat and even becomes a zombies, and now we need to have be ready to fight even with family and watched I think I saw a vampires zombies and they are extremely dangerous and you are really the undead, no matter, being a zombies and get bitten by an ordinary one or not you still become the undead, oh like in the movie night of the living dead? Yep! We need to found out how to killed a thousand but not one by one that will be more harder, yes I know but this the mission and we need to accomplished it now, no one will save us we, that true probably they are alls zombies and we were lucky on the flight and we didn't get bitten or infection by the water, because I didn't drink any, did you? Yes!

I told you not too. But you didn't listen too me, and you could be infection and I will have too killed you, no I will shoot myself when the time comes.

That can happened anytime and I will be alone when you become zombies, and who will help me to shoot them and protection me?

You will be fine, you are a strong lady and I know that you find a safe place went help comes you will be rescue, ok if you says so.

Now you take a left on this light and then a right and the white house and tall fence that is where I use to live with my family and I there is a code that we need to key in and then go in and there are video cameras and electric door open and it was not working at first and then it opened and they both went inside and Kelly called out mom and dad and Kate, where are you? Then Kelly remembers the "secrets room" Kelly wait a minute I am in back of you so where are you going? Upstairs to my parents room and they have a room there and they can be inside there.

Just follow me, ok and are sure that they are there? Yes!

Then Mark said it too quiet here and I don't like it and about two steps more then they saw the zombies, no one what are we going to do? I don't know but we better gets into the room and lock it up, and we will be save there because have electric and have storage with foods and clothes and bed and shower that is great, but we need to get inside now.

Try to walks around them, understanding and tried not let them smell you or you will be a goner, yes, I know Mark, so go for you.

About five minutes later they got inside the room but the secret room was open and now what we might fall into a trap, ok!

Kelly steps inside and then Mark and I felt something on his arm and said did you touch Kelly? No I have not...

No I don't believe this I think that I just got bitten by that man, oh no that is my neighbor Bill and his wife Hazel, and you got bitten and now I will have to shoot you in the head but you should killed them first. Don't worry I think that they didn't bite you but you just hit it on the walls and you are infection, goddess., and I am creepy out of this situation and I wants to make it alive, so do I said Kelly and Mark, and about one hour later, they heard the door bell and then some peoples yelling out and it is Betsy and Bruce and Kelly said I need to let them in and make sure that you close the door behind me, I will and when knock three times then you let me in. ok! I will... they approaching me and I cannot hold them back and I am doing my best said Mark and I am not able to keep them away from us so we need to leaves now, before it is too, you right and know it is dangerous just sit here and do nothing so we better go now and before we are trap inside this mansion and in that secret room, they will break in and we will be dead meat so we can take the Cadillac and drive away in style but will it be fast enough and I can take the corvette and it will be much faster but it is smaller and not so strong has the Cadillac that is true.

So what is the plan Mark so we go into the garage and take that car and drive to the coast of san Diego and then find a safe house for us and then stay there for two days or more and then find a guns and bullets and also find a helicopter to fly out of here, but we been across the country and we still had to deal with zombies., that is true.

We need a better plan do you understand? Do you understand if we don't move quickly and it is air we are dooms, I know so we really don't have a safe place to hide but still we are not infection, that is true so far and I don't know went or if it happened but I hope it does not.

They both got inside the car before that they had to fight off the zombies and she saw her neighbor Bill and he was after her and said I want your brains, and Kelly said start up the car and drive quickly, I am Kelly.

I do not want to be in accident, I know that.

So far we are safe and we have nothing to worry about and we should reach the coast in two hours and I thought it was less, but we are not dealing with freeway and crazy driver, we are on schedule and if we need to fight off the zombies and they don't bite us we will be fine.

On I am going on the 80 route and no car at alls but us.

I think that good sign and we should just watched the exit, that we turned off and then take a left toward the mall and then toward the ocean.

Are sure you know where you are going yes?

Meanwhile back at the house the zombies were surrounded the whole house and few neighbors were not zombies yet but they didn't know how to escape the zombies and what to do!

But Crystal said mom and dad it is time for us to go to the car and driveway and but Crystal and Crystal said that I got a map from map quest and go direct to San Diego to the survivor center and if someone is infection they were help you, how do you know that, by going on the internet, oh I sees, but we are surrounded by the zombies here and we don't have no weapons to killed them off, so we aim toward the head and they will died,, are sure Crystal, yes, you never listened to me, but you should and we should stops argument and leave immediately, ok! Then she steps out and said I think that we should wait what? We need to block up the windows and doors now... they will gets inside, yes. I will!

About one hour later, Kelly and Mark, got to the survivor center and it was like dessert and no one around and this does not looked good I know so what should we do? I don't know that Kelly to Mark...

Mark sat in the car and with Kelly and said we need to leaves because I have a bad feeling and what do you means, I think this place is infection by the zombies and soon has they smell us they will be after us, I don't believe you, and but Kelly got out of the car and looked around and the car and trucks were parked in the back and with a little peek, Kelly notice that Zombies were near by, and then she said to Mark I think that we should leaves now. Then the car were not started up and they were coming in thousands and now Kelly said comes we need to leave I am trying, but it were go, looked at the gauge, and we are out of gas how could you, I was thinking and now we are in danger and we need to find a other car or truck to get way from here, and then they heard the sounds of zombies and someone shooting at them, at this point they didn't know that they were going to runs into Ray, and Ray came up to the car and said we need to go now, but my truck broke down and we are out of the gas, and Mark said where is the nearer gas station and I need to fill up the tank and then we can leave this zone and we can travel north to Seattle, ok! Mark and Ray and Kelly walks to the gas station and had a gas tank container to get some gas and Kelly said how much gas will be gets and how far to we have to walks, about two miles and hope not to run into Zombies, neither, so Kelly slow down and then she saw them coming and said boys! They are coming and Ray started to shoot them in the head and then said I have about ten more bullets and we will not make it, now we need a distract and someone has to be bait, and Kelly said no I am not going…

Kelly said I don't trust you and I think that you should be bait and Ray said do you know how to shoot a gun, of course I do.

Kelly took the gun from Ray and said go ahead and I will make sure that I aim and shoot at those zombies.

Zombies were coming close to Mark and Kelly and almost grab Ray and Kelly shoot and he was dead and Ray said that was a close one and don't miss it, bullets are our lives lines. I do understand.

Touch and Go!

Ray stood and the zombies were coming closer and then Kelly was shooting them and Ray got the gas and ran very quickly and almost drop the gas and Kelly said behind you and Ray said don't worry I have not been bitten yet! That is good but I don't wants to be caught, aim and shoot I am, but you are missing, I know but I am trying my best, I know but let talking and ok! Then she almost shot him and said are aiming at the zombies or are you trying to shoot me, sorry, it won't happen again. About a second later, he was about to be caught, Kelly said watched out they are behind you, and she shoot a few zombies and he was safe and they put the gas into the car and drove way and they were relief.

You never put me in danger again! I do you hears me.

Yes, I do but we needed to be caution and watch where we are going and make sure that we safe and not run into zombies…

At that moment Kelly said to Mark, Ray, watched out Ray a zombies, are in back of you and don't gets bitten, I won't be careful they are about a inch away, and he ran off and he was safe once.

But there a pack are coming toward us I thought we would goner but we are not go they kept going and they got too car and drove away.

About one hour, they got to that town and they reach Disneyland.

Are sure that place will be safe and not sure, then Ray said I will check it out first and sees if it safe, but your not be safe.

So Ray walks around the parking lot and said it is clear and you comes ok we will be coming soon! Kelly and Mark, said follow me I know where I am going and I think that we will be fine, but I have a terrible feeling about this place but we cannot stay here long.

Then Kelly said I will go the different direction but I told her that not walks alone and we need to stick together, but Kelly said I am going alone.

But Mark when after Kelly and Ray was near the roller coaster and walks near the Ferris wheel and said, it is clear here also so are you coming to meet up with me, and no reply so Ray still kept on walking and then he said and called on the cell phone, there are thousand and thousand of zombies here, we need to get away from and he was about to runs and he got caught and bitten on the arms and then he fell to the ground and then Kelly and Mark notice him and he was dragged his body and he tried to warns them, but it was too late.

Mark and Kelly went up to him and said what happened and he was in blood and he couldn't move and seems like he passed out and he died and became a zombies and now Kelly said we better runs and get away from here, I do agree, and Ray was about to grab Kelly leg and Kelly pull out her leg on time and they both ran toward the car and they were behind them, and Kelly said I am scare and so am I said, Ray.

But Kelly fell and Mark pull her up and they ran and ran until they got to the car and the car wouldn't start and I don't like this. I don't neither but we will be fine, so close your windows and door and we will be fine, how do you know, but we were in this kind of situation and we got out and being safe, that is true, but I want to be here now. Then the car started up and they drove away and then they got to the freeway and they headed to San Barbara and so we are not safe anywhere nope!

We don't have any place to go I think I have an idea and it might work and but not sure, ok just I wants a warm place and no zombies around so do I. You think that you are safe but you are not so, but looked around and if is clear then they drove for hours and hours and then Kelly said it will be the same everywhere and the zombies but we need not to take the any faucet water or eat the chicken, because they are bacteria and virus that spread and then you died and then you become a zombies, but I don't know so what do we eat and drink to be safe.

You are scaring me I know but you should face reality and no kidding if we are going to make to tomorrow…

I know that we will and no one will make the different, but we need to find a place to stay to sleep but I am hungry. So am I!

But don't be a wise guy, and so far we are lucky and because we don't know what foods to eat and drink.

Let's stop talking about the zombies and how to get out of this hell, I don't know but we cannot stay in the open because they will sees us and we will not have no place for shelter or they will smell us and they will follows us this that true. Yes, everything that Ray is saying it is true.

I know that, said Kelly, that why I survive this long but I don't wants to brag and runs out of luck neither so we need to go now.

I know but I am exhaust and hungry and dirty and I just want to have a bubble bath and change clothes, so do I.

Then around the corner they when up the hill and Kelly called out and then said I see a house and let go there, ok!

About ten minutes later, they were in the house and then they went inside and then they lock the door shut and try to put on the lights and then the lights they use candle and flashlights and then Kelly said it is a bit creepy here and I don't like it.

Mark said I will keeps you company and Kelly said ok I don't mind if I do.

They left Ray alone to watch the zombies but no trance that night, that what they thought until the rain came pouring down.

Then Kelly said I don't like this, something going to happened soon, what?

About a second later she heard a sound like a banged.

Two minutes later they were inside and then Ray was calling out and said help me and Mark ran out and saw them standing and he called out to Kelly get out and gets dressed now. What? Do you hear what I am saying? Yes they enter the house and we are doomed.

Stops saying that Ray but I am caught in the middle and you are still upstairs and you can escape and I am trap and I have no ways to runs, and I think it might be the end for me and I think just leave me no you are staying with us and I am going to find a weapons to shoot them in the head, so you are willing to died and save my life, maybe lose your own, I don't think so.

Mark said I am not going to save him and risking my own life so I am leaving and so are you Kelly, no, don't be selfish and I think that we can beat them and killed the zombies, are so sure and not thinking that you might be dead meats and become a zombies, no I am a fighter.

Sometime you can lose the fight and then you will be dead, I won't listen to you and you so negative about this, less talking and more fighting get it.

Yes, I do and don't worry in five minutes, I will be torn into pieces and I will fight with my strength and I will never give up.

Fine, once again you are the boss and making the decision for us and I don't like it why don't you shut up and be quiet and fight them off, fine.

At that moment, it was touch and go for them and Ray and said if I was in your place I were have take off and leaves and Mark said, I told you that I didn't trust you so we should have left, I guess you were right.

Stop fighting and need to get them off Ray and I think that they bit him and I think we were stupid to stay here, but we try but now we are stuck here, thanks!

Mark said I can hold them back and you go upstairs and climb out of the window and I will be in back of you.

Will you? Yes don't you trust me; I don't want to be left alone.

You won't promise me, yes I don't lies…

Somehow they manage to escape the zombies once again but they did lost a friend of being careless and Kelly said I will not lose my guard, again do you understand, said Kelly, yes I do…

They climb down from the second floor and got down to the ground and walks toward the road and a speedy car pass them and about two minute later it returned and pick them up and said do you wants a ride to town and Kelly said I don't know, you better says yes! But why, said Kelly because they are coming toward you ok you convince me and we are going with you so what is your name, Jeff, nice too meet you, same here.

Jeff, where did you come from, well I am from San Diego and you far from home, not really, sure but San Barbara is where my family lives.

Oh, I see!

But I thought your home town was San Diego, no I grew up there. But most of my life mostly in Beverly Hills and Hollywood, so I see are a movie star?

I wish, but they there are so many zombies and I don't know where to drive too. But two kind of zombies what? Yes you heard me. I did.

I don't understand what you are saying about zombies.

Two Kinds of Zombies

Wait a minute you are saying two kind of zombies, please explains what you means, well one kind is from the foods and water and the others one are the kind that are bitten by zombies and vampires and the zombies / vampires are the most dangerous one don't you understand? I do but both are dangerous and I don't want to run into them.

I know what will happened well so if you gets bitten by vampires zombies you become a vampires that you sucks blood and you become the undead and ok I still I don't understand the different well if you gets bitten twice by to undead you become more powerful zombies that walks the earth and you wants brains and bloods at the same times. I got it.

Are we going to runs into any here I don't know but I hope not?

But I were not doubt it and I think we are going the right ways do you understand yes but I don't wants to died today or the next days but I hope that we are going far away from them and we can be safe, but having bad feeling we are not still in danger and Jeff was tall blonde and medium build and blue eyes and he was really hot but Mark didn't trust him what he was saying to him, and he tried to warns Kelly not to believe what he was saying, but Kelly was very attractive to him and Kelly tried to get closer but he said not now but when we get to safer location ok! I can do that. But Mark said what are you will getting on with him? No but just being friendly.

Later that night, Jeff was getting tired he stop the car and they sat in the car about one hour and then Mark said I will drive now, but Jeff said you don't know these roads and I do. But I can help out with the driving so you can but not with my car I don't trust anyone driving my car don't you get it, yes I do, said Mark. And he just sat back and was getting angry at Kelly and Jeff, they were started to kiss and hug and Mark was getting jealous at them.

Mark said stop it now we are not safe yet and stop necking and just started driving, I am don't rush me and Kelly was a black hair and short and a little overweigh and Jeff was very attractive to her.

With her smile and Mark was about five feet and five inches tall and he had short hair and a nice smile, but now Kelly was after the blonde. And Mark said I just wants to leave you too lovebirds alone, what are you saying man! So you just wants to get into her pants, well be quiet I will!

But Mark was mad all the ways to San Barbara and then Jeff decided to take a turn into the freeways and what are you doing? Going to universal studio are you crazy I don't wants to go there! We will end up being dead meat, no we will not my uncle bob will have the gun powder and he will blow them away, are you nut Jeff and you are putting us in danger, well you can get out of the car., no thanks!

"SPECIAL REPORT" Zombies spreading quickly of the infection in alls states. Now what are we going to do? I don't know. But we cannot stay here that true, but Mark he doesn't realize that we will be in big trouble if we go his direction but I need to mention it too him and I think that you are right! But then Jeff said what are you saying, you don't listen to me and you think that I am wrong, how you are so whine and I don't wants to hears this again, so far from your uncle bob about two miles from Universal and do you think that he is alive, yes but we don't have to go inside his driveway, but we are not staying unprotect do understand we are going inside with you, fine, why are you making this has a federal case out of this and we will beat those zombies and once again Mark said big talk and little action, and you better shut up your mouth before I shut up for you.

Fine,, but this is crazy idea to go to your uncle house and we can be trap and we can become dead meat and then Jeff said get out of my car this instantly said Jeff to Mark, and don't get to hasting, ok!

Then Kelly spoke and said stop fighting and gets along and don't you know being in a group your survive is more better in chance you don't says said Jeff so how did you become so expert with the chances of beating the zombies,, I been in a few fight and I still could talking about it, that true so how long you are lucky? I don't know I will not give up.

Then Jeff and Mark and Kelly got to his uncle place and said I don't understand that the fence is open and what do you think that the zombies are inside I think that might be so be on guard and if they try to bite you so you hit in the head and hope that are dead, into the brains.

I got it Jeff and now I think that Mark was right that we should have kept going toward the south and you took us here, ok now you are taking his side.

No, I am thinking maybe we took the wrong choice and I don't regret it.

Sorry, said Jeff to Kelly I never wanted to put us into danger, and then should sees how your uncle is and hope that he is not a zombie.

I hope not., and then they were going on the path and he saw his uncle coming up to him and thought he was fine but the closer that he got and he said go back and why? He is infection what?

She called out and said Jeff don't get bitten, I won't.

Be careful and I will and Mark said I am going back to the car and I am going back with you too and Jeff said wait for me too. I will.

Mark and Kelly ran back and Kelly was looking back and said hurried.

But then Jeff was left behind and I don't sees him and I will go back, no I will no you are staying with me, so we both will go back ok!

That is a bad ideas you stay in the car and being helpless no ways! I am not staying alone I am going with you, ok fine!

Meanwhile Jeff was trying to fight off his uncle and then he notice blood on his arms and said, next I will become one zombies and Jeff pull out a knife and stab him in the head and fell down to the ground and died. You must be kidding me that there are two kind of zombies, no I am not we need to stick together and get the hells of out here, do you understand Mark and but we need to save Jeff but it is too late for him, we have to try and I am not risking my life to save him, don't have anything are cold like ice no! But I am thinking how to stay alive, well you are being selfish maybe I am but I don't wants to died here, I don't neither. So we are going and we will not get killed and we will survive this nightmare, but we are not stand around and time click ticking and ticking, so let go now.. Ok. Now Kelly and Mark, and Jeff is gone and now we need to move and not too good back.

Maybe we can take him to that medical clinic to cure him, but that too late, maybe it is not too late, don't stall let go and move quickly and quiet.

They move through the woods and the terrain and the water near that bridge, they cross it and walks further, and future.

Then Kelly and Mark stops and relaxing and drinking a lot of water and then Mark, vomit and Kelly said what happened I don't know.

You should drinking the water and I am and then he just fell down and Kelly and went up to him and try to wake him, then he woke up and then said how long was I out.

About five minutes later, Mark got up and I am feeling fine and are you able to walks and I called out and he was deep in the woods and I called out but Mark stops and I caught up to him, and I seen in his eyes and it was not same and now I am afraid.

But I just didn't stand too close to him, because he was acting totally different and I didn't want him to notice I was not the same.

Then Mark said what wrong? Nothing, but are you afraid of me.

No, but closer ok I am and I got closer and I notice his teeth, and the green eyes now I knew I was in danger but I still stay and I was really fearful and I didn't know what will happened to me and I knew that I cannot drink that bottle water if I do I will become infection and turn into a monster, and I was silent and I watched how he change in moment and I knew that I need to find a gun and shoot him but I didn't find a gun but I knew that I needed to hit his head and cut it out, and I knew it were be not be easy and he stops and said " Go away from me now" why?

I am changing and I will become a zombies, and I don't wants to hurt me but you promise that you were not leave me, but I just did a mistake and I drank the water and I didn't know this was going to happened to me.

I am sorry, Kelly but please leave me now, I wants to helped you but you cannot and just runs for your life, I have the urge to eat your brain.

So I started to runs and out of breathe, then I saw a car coming along and at that moment it stops and I walks up the car and said do you wants a ride, and I said sure I do! I got inside and then he said my name is Ben and what is your name and I said Kelly and nice too meet you.

Ben and Kelly Journey

Same here and I am glad that you came and I am all alone in these woods and there are many zombies around here and we need to keeps driving and I think that we should get to Las Vega, Nevada, are sure, yes there is a safe house and we should go there, looked out, here comes the zombies and they are very quick, and I should be driving much quicker and I will not stop unless we need gas for the car and it is really dangerous and risking to stop and you probably know that all ready so how long were you out here? Probably a week, and you didn't get bitten I need to check your whole body, what? Yes I don't need to carry a infection bitch in my car, why with his fowl language, well these days you don't know if your going to make it, or not but I don't wants to died today by picking you up. Ok check me out mister and I have nothing to hide, good girl.

Fine, so he slow down and stop the car near the wooden area and said step out and I need to check you out and so Kelly said fine!

At that moment he pull her to the ground and pull off her blouse and pants and underwear and then he put his finger into her vagina and said to finger fuck her, and at that moment I said stop this and he refuse and he pull out his dick and put inside and holding her tight and that Kelly couldn't fight and then he got up and got dress and said now we can go.

But Kelly lies on the ground naked body and he pull her up and threw her in the back of the car and her clothes and then started up the car and drove away, and Kelly lies in the back seat of her car and cried and he said you are no virgin but you are some good piece of ass and I will get more later, and she looked at him and saw a weapon in back seat and was about to hit him and then the zombies were coming toward them and she just lies back and waited for the right moment to hit him and get away.

They drove toward the Seattle but Kelly didn't say anything but quiet and then he pull over and said I want to fuck you again and again, Kelly.

But she refuses to looks at him and he said can I have you again?

Then she said you force me and now you are asking me after you rape me, how could you? I am sorry and we are going through times and I am confuse and I loss someone that I loved and I am lonely and I do desire your love, you mean sex? No both! Fine, I did lose someone special myself but I don't rape anyone, I wants to apology again too you, I don't know what exactly I did but I am sorry, ok! Then they got close and he hug her and kiss her lips and once again they had sex and it was good and Kelly said if you asked I were not says no because you are very sexy and hot.

Then he hold her and said we cannot stay here long, I believe these woods have a lot of those zombies around.

It was getting lighter outside and now it is time that we need to leave, ok! Then Kelly got dress and so did Ben.

They drove for hours and hours and then they final they got to "Seattle" and Kelly said is this a good place to go I am not sure but my friend Ken, will help him out and he has a high rise building and a bunker that we can be safe and not runs into zombies. Oh I see, I am not sure about anything that goes on in the world.

This day! No I am not being abuse by you or anyone else what she said, but do think that Ken is lives, I don't know. But we are still lives and they might be zombies, at this point I don't know.

We will be there in half hour and his house is on left and the red house and with the picket fences around, yes I listened too you and I hope that is not a pert and I am not going to gets rape by your friend Ken? No I don't think so, but you don't know, that is true and it was getting late and it was getting dark and then Kelly looked up and said looks that moon and it is so big and bright and I know. Then the rain started and Kelly said that is a not a good sign because when the rain fall the zombies do comes.

About ten minutes later, they reach the house but it was in flames and saw someone coming out from the yard and it was Ken, but he didn't looked the same and I think that he became a zombies and I think that I am a mistake and I think that we should leave now so where should we go. Then he drove likes a crazy man and Kelly said stops driving like that way we will end up in crash and then we will get eaten up by the zombies and then we will become zombies well you talked to much be quiet I am

Jean Marie Rusin

trying to think fine! Kelly just sat there and thought and then he said we are going to Detroit Michigan, you must be kidding no I am not! My friend Raymond lives there and it is cold there and we should be safe from the zombies, but you don't have the clues how it is spread and it is by the water and the certain foods that you eat and that cause the disease, that the peoples change into the zombies. I don't believe you, but it causes it.

Then Ben stops the car and told Kelly, gets out of car, no are you crazy?

I Said no but Ben push me out of car and I hurt my knee on the sidewalk and he drove away, I was standing on the sidewalk, but then zombies would coming, I didn't know which ways to runs, but I ran into the first house that saw and I lock the door, and I looked around, seem strange no one around and then suddenly Ruby was in the room.

Then Ruby follows me and hid in the closet, and then she opens the door and at that moment I didn't know what to do.

Then Ruby came up too me I thought she was going to bite me but she hug and didn't let me go. So I walks out and hold her hand and then I took her to the kitchen and asked if she wants some food and she nodded her head and then Kelly looked into her eyes and then I notice that she is changing in front of me, I just like froze but I had a antidote and I gave Ruby shot and she just fell down to ground and then she got up and she was normal, then I looked her, and I said do you want something like nuggets, no I don't like but that is fatting foods and I want a pizza, yes I do, I don't know I can gets a pizza, about a second later, someone just came in and I was still standing, but we are not going out there and they could be waiting for us and we can be eaten or bitten and turn into a zombies, no ways! But the little girl "Ruby" still was yelling and screaming and Ruby was about to walks out of the room and open the door and was about to steps out and then Kelly ran up to her and said don't do it.

You are risking ours lives and I don't wants to dies today or tomorrow do you understand what you are saying. Yes I do Kelly, so we need to be very careful and not to go outside and gets bitten, you are just repeating yourself and so my parents are gone and my little brother is also gone, he got caught by the zombies and he became one instantly and I am alone in the world but you are not, I meant to says that my family is gone and now I am orphan and I have no one at alls.

That is not true, you have us and you can be our family so what happened when the zombies bite you and you are gone and how will I survive and I don't want to be alone. Then Ruby ran into the bathroom and then tries to climb out of the window and at that moment I caught her and then, Mark said what are you doing? Looking for my family, are you suicide no but I do miss them very much, so do I said Kelly but I don't go out and risk other people and I am not but I don't like it here.

But explains why? Because they did get inside here and I think that they will do it again, you think that they are gone, but they are really around the corner and they will grabbed you and bite you and you fall to the ground and your dead, and then you gets up and you are undead.

I don't wants to listen to this said, Ruby no I don't but if you think that we should leave we will go! About someone listen to me and I did warn my family and then they avoid me and now they are dead.

Kelly went up to Mark and said we need to go right now and I think that we should go, and Ruby said who are you talking too, there is no one but you and me, what are you saying, it you and me, about my friend Mark.

There is no one else but us, I don't believe you looked in front of you do you sees anything one? No! Am I losing my mind?

You are too stressed and you are confused and your friends are dead and we are the only two left.

Kelly walks into the bedroom and saw here family slaughter.

We must go now and so I will get the car and I will get you near the door and we will leave Seattle and head to Michigan, but why?

It is a safe zone and I think it is safe I am not sure.

I don't want to leave Seattle, we need to leave and I believe that we will be safe in Michigan, but there could be zombies too, I know but we cannot stay here, we will get bitten and I don't have no more antidote.

I don't want to become zombies because of so many years that I fight and I don't wants it end now. Do you understand Ruby?

Yes I do and let go now and don't looks back, don't even looks at family.

Long Journey

Ruby and Kelly left Seattle and headed to Michigan and so what part are we going because my grandmother lives in Grand Rapid, so I think that we are going there, not sure at this moment.

So they both were in the car and drove off into the highway and drove and drove for hours and hours and didn't make any stops.

Until they got to border of Seattle, and they could stops and said I am weak and I cannot go on said Ruby what do you mean I think that antidote didn't work and I am changing quickly, no I cannot believe it.

Then Kelly looked at Ruby and said child I think that I need to killed you and Ruby said don't tell me and then a police car came and stops and the police officer grab Kelly hand and said you were going to killed this child. You are under arrest and I have take you and then about one minute later she was about to bite the officer, then Kelly grab the gun from Ryan and shot Ruby in the head. And Ryan said you save my life and I was going arrest you so forget about this incident and like it never happened. So what really happened you shot a little girl and you don't have doesn't have a feeling on your face like she didn't mean anything.

But I when through a lot with zombies and I believe that if I don't I will died. And end of story, ok I am not against not dying and fighting for your life that is all about it. So let leave now and go toward to grand rapid and I said fine. About one hour later they were there and Kelly said sure it looked a nice place and I were not mind to settle down and rest and take a shower, and sleep in a bed and not being a afraid of being infection or someway, so I just wants to play it safe and I what do you think.

Went we find a place, make sure that the car is park near by that in case if we needed too getaway, I totally agree, yes.

They got into the city and there were many hotel and many peoples on the sidewalks and bags and little children playing and then they when up a few roads near the hospital and it was dark and no one around and then Kelly said to Ryan we should go back and I don't like this spot and he turned around the car and then he saw a little girl calling out and Kelly said don't stops just keeps going and He said why?

I don't like it, and I had a intuitive about this and I think that she is a zombies and I need to know if she is not a zombie and you are going to risk your life yes because I am a police officer and that is my job.

Fine! But don't take too long and I will wait for you in the car, she might be afraid of me, well you wanted to stops so I am not going I refused don't you understanding, yes I do and I am not moving, ok!

Meanwhile Kelly sat in the car and looked and then saw what was going on and then Kelly step out and said Ryan I am coming and he called out and said "stay in the car" but why and he said I don't want anything happened too you.

Something is wrong? I don't think so! But why I do want to helps, I hear sounds and they are coming this ways. Ok!

I will go back to the car and I will lock it up until you come back.

Good idea and I will be there soon, and about a second she heard a shot and then I pop out of head and saw him lying on the ground and I saw the little girl, and coming me but she had some blood from her face, and I when on the driver side and I drove away, and I didn't looks back.

I have loss a lot of my friends and I don't want to have this sad feeling again! I just wants everything to be normal has before and not so many tragedy, and mayhem this must end, I agree said Ryan but looking back don't but it will not just go away but less pain. But this is not the end of road. I don't know if we will make so I want make it and but we don't make it so let make love right. So Ryan to my hand and we went inside the car and that night we make passion love and then, we surrounded by zombies, now what? I don't know...

One hour later, we would stick inside the car not sure if the car.

I really don't know we cannot gets out of car no we will gets bitten.

No, we need to be quiet, I am quiet... ok what next.

I don't know but we need to go now... Yes start up the car.

But I am trying to but the car won't start, the window got smash and the glass, into the car, one of zombies and almost grab my hand and Kelly pull my hand, I felt a bit on the hand.

You save me and I could become zombies, but I am not infection.

Are sure yes I am? Kelly said I will look at your arm again!

Once again somehow I started up the car and knock down a few zombies down and headed on the highway toward Chicago.

About two miles you we near Chicago, and Ryan started too weird.

No, then Kelly got out the antidote and gave the shot to him and he fell in the backseat and fell sleep and slept for hours.

Then he woke up and he got refresh and normal and he was ready and said I drive now, so I stop in the middle of road and I got out and we switch place and then we drove over the bridge.

Once we got there, then we would in Chicago, and I asked maybe we will have some stuff pizza, and then we got in the middle of city.

The lights would out and then we saw burning car and splatter bodies, and I said we need to go now.

So once he started up the car and then he put the lights on the car and we saw thousand zombies and now what?

Ryan drove away but we got to the crossing and we would block in and at that moment, and then he looks at me but now he was acting a little strangely, no you are not turning I am feeling funny, you are making me worry, I will be fine, so I think the antidote is working and effect my brain and then he stop talking slowly.

Then Ryan was fine and kisses her lips and they drove off and cross the bridge. Two hours later, they would toward New England, so we will be going to Worcester, Mass, are you should yes.

I think that great idea I don't think so. We will sees went we gets there no matter how it turned out we will be safe and takes my word and I will and we will be the only survive of this terrible accident with the water and foods virus, and alls foods are not effect when it happened couples year ago, no one didn't have the clue until now and but no one is getting the right dose of the antidote and I think sometime it does work, when I took it work right oh way! But now when I gave other person they somehow became zombies, but I don't know about you so far it is working but I need to sees if you will have to get another shot and it will be make you not sick and you will be alive.

But it is no will be sick again and become a zombies, but I believe that you will be not effect and you will become healthy. But it will be a lost progress and I am glad that I save you, Ryan said I am too.

Later that night the storm came in when they were driving to Worcester but they didn't end up there just kept on driving and driving and we end up in New York city and how did we do that's ? I don't know but this are our destiny and that does not changing, but we are not going there neither so we will go to Atlantic City and we will try the trump casino.

But what happened if the broad walk is with zombies so we will deal with that when it happens but otherwise we will be fine.

Ok! But don't gets paranoid ok I won't and they kept driving and then the car stall and Kelly said I guess we are out of gas and we need to fill up now if we going too make our last journey, so said it will be the last?

I am not and I am not going to give up, at that moment there were thousand zombies headed there ways and Ryan said run for your life and don't looked back, I won't!

Ryan said I will try to beat them and Kelly said are you crazy? No but someone has to survive this awful circumstance, well I thought we both were do that's, but you need to find a safe place and I will try not to get bittern, but I cannot use the antidote, because that is the ways it will not work over and over, so be careful I will said Ryan.

At the last moment he decided to runs and catch up to Kelly and said I am not going to risk my life and we need to find a place to stay but we are in the middle of the highway and there are no houses but woods in front of us and we have no water or foods and we are going to gets weak and we are going to dies and no one will save us.

I don't want to hear what you are saying but this is the truth and just face it, I will!

No, I am fighter once I been a cop and the force got killed off by zombies and when things get back to normal, I will be a police officer.

Law and serve and yes and that what I am doing with us.

Antidote not working

Two hours that night Ryan said something is wrong with me and I cannot explain it but I cannot be near you, but why?

Don't you see it in my eyes and at that moment I looked at his eyes and I backed away and said I need to stay far away from you Ryan?

No, help me, I cannot I gave you many doses and it is not working on you and the system is not accept it so, when you change I need to shoot you in the head, and I will make sure that I am not effective no way.

I thought you were helping me, but I did but didn't work on you because it went into your blood system. I don't want to listen what you are saying about me, you are scaring me, I don't wants to but it is true, sorry, my new friend. I gave you the right dose and it not working because it could been switch at the lab where I took it and I had some and it work and I don't understand Ryan, but your body could be very bad effective by the virus and I gave it too you too late., you are saying that I am going to be a zombie? I think you are and I cannot help you but I will shoot you if I needed too. Thanks a lot I think that you make it happen, how I am not the one but I told you not to drink the faucet water and you did and then you ate that watermelon and that effective the system and I cannot do anything about that. You need to give me one more shot, well I only have one left and it mine, don't be selfish help me now. Then he pull out the gun and was about to shoot me but I somehow bend down at that moment and I was not shot, and he ran out of bullets but he alerts the zombies to comes this ways and I was so furious with him so I locked him up in the closet and he was screaming and yelling and the zombies were coming closer and I was terrify about that.

Ryan was banging and shouting and I told him to be quiet and he didn't listen to me and I thought to myself this could be the end for me.

But I thought to myself and I am not giving up and I am going too fight.

It is about two hour later, Ryan stopping make noise in the closet and I check on him and he looked fine and I took him out and wake him up and said, so you are lucky and he just started to wake up and said what do you mean? You are fine and you didn't change into a zombie and the shot help you out and he smiled and said thanks, Kelly.

But then I looked again but I knew that I was wrong he will become a zombie and I let him in the room where I am and I definite will become dead meat, somehow I try to move far from him and he started to asked me question and said are you afraid of me? Nope! So why are you so far from me? I just wants to looks out and when we need to leave but I didn't want him too get suspicious and I didn't wants to be weird and acting different too him to give my self away, so I was silent and friendly at the same moment.

I stood still and I didn't says anything but I stood still like I was froze and then I notice the change in his face and his speak and now I knew that I had to runs out of that place but also knew that there a lot of zombies outside and neither I get bitten by him or the one outside, this scenario I had no choice but leave and then Ryan said where are you going I wants to eat your brain, and I hit him on the head and I open the door that I didn't even realize until they came closer too me and I knew this could be the end for me, but I still fight and knock some of them on the ground.

I when toward the car and I start it up and I headed toward Atlantic City, New Jersey, and I really drove away so quickly and I didn't looked back to Ryan because he is one of them, and I am the only survivor that I know that I am.

I kept on driving and driving and I knew that I was getting weaker and weaker and I knew that I had to take the last of the antidote, and I was not feeling good like the last time that I took the dose and I believe that some tamper with the antidote, and I was driving and falling the sleep.

I knew that I had to stop, if I didn't I were crash and burn and I were end up being dead and I didn't wants to died today.

Now the night is here and I was still on the road and I didn't sees the highway and I stop and then a second later, I saw them coming and I drove quicker and quicker and then I got to the "Washington bridge" at that moment. There were thousand and thousand on the bridge and then I need to pass the them and I don't know if I am going to make it.

At that moment I pray alls the ways the cross and about ten jump on the car and I somehow shook them off but mores were coming toward me and at that moment I thought that the car were go into the river.

But I somehow got control and drove away and at that moment I was relief and didn't look back.

Then suddenly I stop and got out of the car and I thought it was bit stupid to do that but I didn't was alone and I was tired and I need some fresh air and I smell the smoke air and I now I went back to the car and I felt a weak and then I kept driving until I got to trump casino.

I park the car in the garage and took the elevator and when on the lower floor and then I walks around and around and then I sat down and then I saw a lady coming toward me and said go away now!!!

You are in danger and they are in here but she ran into the elevator and ten of the zombies caught her and she was gone.

I got up and I looked two both sides and then I walks very slowly and then I when toward the dead person and I wipe her blood and sweat on my clothes and walks like a zombies and somehow I mange to get out of there alive, and I was relief I thought I was safe but I was wrong.

Somehow they smell me and I was close to the car and then the car were not start up and I was scared.

About ten minute later, I heard someone shooting and then he came and he was tall and blonde and he was slim and sexy and he came to the car and he said, ,my name is Jack, so what is your name? Kelly.

Nice too meet you Kelly under this circumstance, I know so we need to head out of here immediately, yes I know. Then he spoke softy and he was nice kind and he knew what to do and he looked at me and I knew that he was attractive to me, so was I to him.

About two minute later, his friend John came along and now I was not alone but some two strong men with guns, and zombies behind us.

At this point I really didn't trust them I knew that I was not complete safe with them but I kept quiet and I just drove away from that place and headed on the highway and I just drove, and then John said, you look like a California girl, well I am and I am far way from home since the virus spread coast to coast, sure I do understand, but a lot of our friend dies because the virus and I think that we should head toward to South Caroline, and I think that is a mistake there is no safe haven from the zombies, I think you are right but we need to find a location.

Yes we need to lodge and then keeps going and no stopping.

But we also got to rest or we will get so tired that we will make a mistake and end up dead and I don't think so.

So I am taking your opinion and I think that you can be wrong about your decision and so far I kept you alive and you are still nagging and I still am alive from the first incident, from long times ago and you don't know what I went through making it this far and it was not a easy task too take and there were a lot of journey that I took and I make it and this will not be the end of me do you understand? John and Jack and don't be in my ways. Yes we do and we follow yours rule and we will beat this virus.

We will be there in less than one hour and half and we will sees what going on there and we need a plan of escape in case we runs into zombies, so I am glad that you are on your toes and I am not the only one that has to figure out a plan and shoot those bastard in the head and I don't want to be dead meat or walks like a zombies, and be dead.

We got it said Jack and John and we will do what you said and mores.

So we will survive this nightmare and tells our grandchildren and they will tell there, I hope so. I don't have no negative thought in my mind and I believe that we will be safe and we will not get bitten and it is like a few year that I been killing those zombies and my friend that helped me he got killed in the last journey.

Just paid attention and the area less popularity and we need to go there I believe that we won't get the zombies.

But I am not sure about anything at this point do you know what I am saying, yes and so we still heading south to South Carolina

Won't the zombies come out of the ocean or the river and the lakes I don't know, but from ocean I can says yes!

Destination

The winds were blowing and the waves were getting higher and the storm was coming in the from the ocean and we would driving near the coast and we saw them coming out of the water and I told John and Jack we should get away from the coast, then I started to speed up the car and then I didn't know that was a cliff coming up and then I suddenly stops on the edge of that road and I was terrify what just happened and I thought I was losing it but then I said no we need to go on and find more survive and rescue them and take them with us but one thing that I am out the antidote and I will not be able to help anyone now. Unless that we go to that lab in Maryland, Baltimore, where the government has hidden from us, so Kelly are so resources and helpful I know, but you need to keeps it a secrets do you gets it, yes we do Kelly. Times when by I knew that we should not stay there for hours and just looks for supplies and leave and but John and Jack had different ideas and once they tried to take my car keys and leave me that how I felt but I was on the watched and also be careful with the zombies, that they could be coming and we need to find a place to sleep and eat, somehow we find a restaurant and it was dessert and so we when inside then the "Special Report" came on and said don't eat the peanut butter or the grape jelly because it is affect with the virus and don't drink the tap water, and there are more warning, yes they are, don't eat everything that you sees it might be affect with the virus, I know. Then John when inside the kitchen and pick up some carrot stick and then he find some lettuce and Kelly said don't eat it, I did, you stupid fool, we need to read what is affect and what we can eat.

I was hungry, so I ate it and I feel fine, we will know in one hour if you have the virus and I hope I don't have it, otherwise we will have too shoot you.

Don't threaten me, I will be fine! So they alls sat at the table and watching John but seems fine and then John got up and he was about to go the kitchen and was about to drink some tap water and Kelly came up and said are you crazy too drink the water. Are you nuts and she said go ahead and do it, so he just was about too take a sip so he stop, I don't want to be paranoid, fine!

Now it was about two hours later after dinner and John said I think that I have a stomach ache something I ate so I need to lay down, and now Kelly said we need to watch him, but why? His first sign of the illness, you getting sick and I cannot even help you John but I will have to killed you went you become a zombies, it will not happened and I didn't drink a lot of that water and I will flush it out of my system, are you crazy no one can do it and you will not make it and I should shoot you now.

Why can you help him said Jack, because he pollute himself by drinking the water and that will make him become a zombie and you wants to save him unless it he had the powerful antidote and then he probably were make it but not in his case and I am not going to died because of his careless, do you understand? Yes John just went into the corner and said we need to find a medical faultily and then I can get medical help, that true. But time is running out by the minutes by saving him, do you understand Jack to John I do but still wants to help him, well I loss a lot of friends of this virus and I am not going to loss my life because him being jerk and putting us in danger. I know but don't get bend out of shape and we will make it and don't think the worst about anything but just let keeps on going and we will make our destiny and we will be fine and we will be cure, how do you know that's? I don't know but the government might screw us and we still can become zombies, so you are blaming the government for this? Yes I am. So I don't believe the negative about what you are saying? But we need to stick together and we will survive this ordeal, once again you are trying to make me feel happy and safe.

Go I will listened to your advice and I hope we will not be dead and also do not drink the water from the faucet, because the virus is in that water and you gets affective and you died and you become the undead zombies, but you also mention the other zombies and they are vampires/ zombies and they are really the vicious and predict where they might strike and you are dead and then you have fang and then you wants brains, and you are so deadly and dangerous species of alls.

71

It is a long times that I didn't sees those species and I don't wants to runs in any zombies at alls.

So Kelly you are open and being honest how you are feeling and how you survive. Yes I know! But I don't want to talks about it anymore, do you understand? Later that night they were driving and driving and then they had to find a gas station and Kelly said we should stops and rest and have a good night sleep, and John and Jack said we need to get to the border of Connecticut first.

We are there yet? No, but pretty soon and I think we should not stop in Connecticut and we should go back to Manhattan and we should head to Atlantic City, and Jack said ok! They got to Connecticut, and there were no virus in that state so Kelly said let head to Manhattan, New York, are you sure? Yes! I want to know if the city is clear and the government got rid of them, ok!

Meanwhile John was acting a bit under weather and I said to him, what wrong, John? I am fine…

John was getting pale and fragile and I knew that moment he was going to died; somehow I knew that I had to kill him before he killed us.

What are you doing and Jack pull the gun away from me and I said I guess you have a death wish, what are saying at that moment, John was really getting to his color of being a zombie and looks into his eyes and Jack looks and then he pull the trigger and he was dead and now what? So we dump him on the side of the road, I think so!

"Staying Alive"

Do you think that we should take him to a funeral home and leave him there? There is no funeral home anymore, Jack, just zombies that wants our brains; I guess you have not learned anything yet!

Yes I loss my friend that I knew from high school and I shot him in the head because he turned into a zombie. I have an enough pain, and loss right now and we didn't help him but killed him so you prefer him killing us?

I thought we would reach the faculty and we would have save him but time just ran out for him and I did warns him about the water, seems like you have no heart, but I do. I am very sorry about your friend, but we didn't reach the place and I don't have one but probably gone, I think that you are right! But you don't have agreed with me. But I am.

Later that night Jack and I got closer and then he gave me a kissed and I cuddle near him at the rest stop at that moment we didn't sees anymore zombies so far.

Then we left the rest stop and headed toward Manhattan. New York and I knew this place was being different, and not safe but danger area. So we making the right decision going to the city where there are many thousand of zombies and we don't have the gunpowder too killed them alls, I know, so I think we should just turn back and go someplace else and we probably would not died today!

But there are many zombies every where and we have no place too go and we need to beat and stay alive, and not think that we will died.

On the special report bullet said they we will be releasing missiles to the target of the zombies and Kelly said to Jack we need to leave and I don't want to die today! We won't we need to cross over and not to be a target and gets killed so runs very quickly and pray too god but they are coming closer to us, I don't have the energy to runs, then Jack fell and Kelly called out to him and then the missiles fell down and the everything got bright and then they both lays on the ground and hold each others hands and then it stops and then Kelly got up and saw the smoke and Kelly couldn't breathe and Jack barely got up, and said what happened? Then tanks and military came and they were about too shoot and then they looked into our eyes and they knew that we were fine… and they took us to the hospital and gave us test and we were not allow to leave the area until it was safe, but Jack said I have a plan too how too escape, I don't like that's!

Two hours later Jack escape from the military and when into the zone and about two hours he been shot, to be presumed of being a zombies.

Meanwhile Kelly stay at the camp and ran into Ray and said I didn't know that you join the service and he walks her into his room and they talked and they make love that night, and said I will protection you.

Listens I survive and loss a lot of my friends and I know that I will make it further, but I will be there for you… the lighted when out and Kelly said what going on? We are being attacked by the zombies. And the battle will begin… and everything got silent… then a voice and banged and booms, and it stops, battle begins now… no, yes! So what should do now I don't know but we cannot stay here we need to leave her right now!

Kelly and Ray started to runs but they didn't have no place to hide but they kept on running and at that moment Kelly said I don't have the energy to run but I need to rest and Ray said if you stops… you will end up being dead meats. It will not happened and I am not going to died today I am going, lives and we will beat the odd of dying so I do believe you so we need too go now, said Ray. Ok I am coming so do you what spread the virus, well not exactly but I think it is airborne I cannot gets the virus, don't breathe it in I won't. Kelly was a relief for a while and then she said it is possible to gets the virus so far we didn't drink the water from the faucet but the bottle water is so far safe, but I am not sure about anything. But the zombies are following us, and that is not good for us no it is not… I agree and we are not safe anything and the sun are shiny and I hope that we get away from here and find a safe heaven.

About one minute later the earth move and then it got dark and we didn't sees anything then we heard them coming closer. I think one of the m is standing next too me and no, yes but don't let it bite me.

Promise that when I turned into zombies shoots me in my head and dons t hesitates about it. I won't I will shoot. And do the same to me, I will said Kelly too Ray, but we do have a battle to fight and win, yes we do.

At that moment, Kelly breathes and then she was relief, and I didn't get bitten but we need to be silent and be quiet when we move through the zombies, ok.

Then the rain came down and they walk very slowly, and then they passed the thousand of zombies and then the lights came on and then the zombies saw they and they ran so fast and I am not going too stop and I am going to survive this nightmare, so am I.

Hope that we do and I hope that we will be save but so far I know that we are on our own and I don't know what I am saying.

That is true! But we need to continue running and we don't have a minute to stops so we better not rest until we are safe and no more zombies that are dreams that possible might comes true.

Then she kiss him and said to him I don't wants to be alone tonight I wants you too be with me tonight, I will be.

But first we need to go find a safe place too goes and then we can be together and not too be afraid of anything anymore, I know.

But please hold me, I will and don't let me go! But we need to go and we will be there dinner and you don't wants that don't you?

They both got walks and walks to end of the street. Then they stops!

Night of Passion

They walks inside and they locked the doors and then I heard that some sound and I thought the military came but I was wrong it was the zombies having guns and shooting so we locked the doors and windows and sat quietly and then Ray came to me and kiss my lips and I kiss him back and he took his shirt and then he remove my blouse and he kiss me and I lay on the floor and Ray was on top of me and I just wanted to kiss him alls over and then I was laying naked on the floor and he was on top of me and he make me feel so good and he was inside of me.

I was moaning and making sound and I was happy at that moment and then I said to Ray I heard a crack and I was right and one of the zombie got inside the building and then Ray ran up and got the shot gun and shot the zombies in the head and then Ray got some more woods and block it and then once again the zombies enter the building and Kelly started to scream and Ray ran for the shotgun and started to shoot and some of the zombies got back up and once again, he fired the shot and ran into the other room with Kelly and said I only have two bullets, so instead of killing the zombies, maybe we should killed ourselves, and Kelly said are give up, I thought you were stronger but not weakly.

He approach and wanted to kiss her and Kelly said get away from me.

Why are you acting like this, I thought you wanted to lives but when it gets a little difficult, you give up and I am not like this.

So I am going too died and I am going to gets out of here with you and myself, and I am going to find a place to be safe without zombies.

But Kelly I am not giving up but I just don't wants to be bitten by them and become one, I don't neither.

They stay in that room and then Kelly notice that there was a back door and she whisperer to him and said "follow me" and he just looked at her and follow her and they walks out in the back door and then Kelly saw the car and it was still running and Kelly said, get inside and we can leave this terrible place and we just got to drive and drive until we know that we will not be invaded by the dead.

Also I heard that the undead are two types and one are from the virus and the other one are vampires / zombies.

The vicious one is the zombies / vampires type they are the one that suck your blood and eat your flesh.

Ok! But both are very dangerous and they want our brains.

About two hours later, they stop at the motel near the Lakeview.

Do you think that we can stay here? I think so, do we check in I guess so.

They walk inside and they looked around and it didn't look good and then Kelly said I have a bad feeling about this place.

"What are you saying"? Well we are not alone here! Ok! Got what you're saying!

Now what well, we cannot stick around here but we need to get into the car and leaves, sure I am going and then Kelly said well maybe we should looked around, I think that is a bad idea, me too! Then they got into the car and then Kelly said looks they are coming!!! I see them. Move it now.

But the car wouldn't start and then it did.

They drove out of the parking lot and kept on going until the gas ran out and they landed at a river view and it was near the ocean.

Now what stay here and wait for someone to rescue us and it can takes days and days and even month and the zombies can just comes and bite us and we will turn and I will not wait to be killed I refuse do you understand Ray. Then he came close to Kelly and embraces her and kisses her neck and then took her hand and walks into the room and lay her down and Ray was on top of her. He kissed her and then they heard a banged and said did you hear that? No we are fine! I don't think so think that we should stop and leave, no we are staying. Ok! About a moment later, about twenty of the zombies came inside the room and Kelly screams and knock off Ray and pick up the gun and started to shoot and then no more bullets, and now what? Just runs and go to the car and let leave, fine and he got dress up in hurried and one of the zombies grab his arms and Kelly pull him and they ran quick to the car and knock down a few zombies and got inside the car and drove away.

That was a close call and then Kelly said well we left ours supplies and we are dooms! We will find some supplies and we will be fine. I don't know where we are at this moment, but we will make it.

They drove all night and then stop at a motel and it looks like it wasn't invaded by zombies and walks into the lobby and check in and got the room and but they heard sound and it really got louder and louder and they came into the parking lot and I said looked they are here too and we cannot stay here, we need to leave, so how do we get out, I don't know.

Ok , the plan is run out and get into the car and drive away, sure it sound easy just talking about it but there are hundreds and we don't have anything to killed them, so don't get bitten, that alls it counts.

When I count to three we run out and keeping running to the car and leave, ok also fighting them off you, and what?

I am going to open the door and follow me and give me the keys and I will drive the car up too you, that is totally risking and I wants to go with you but it you gets bitten and I will be a goner, and I do need the keys, give them to me, fine! What happened if you get bitten, I am dooms!

Think positive and we will be fine, I need to go now or we will be surrounding by thousand and thousand of them. Go now I will!

Kelly was about to steps out and snuck between the zombies and slowly reach the car and open it and Ray called out behind you, what?

Kelly got inside and saw that zombies was about to bite her, she kick him down and started up the car and drove right in front of the motel and Ray came out and then they were coming!!!! Now what? I don't know just keep on driving and don't stop and I won't stop until we get to ours destination, fine! Good I cannot wait to get there and hope it is safe.

We drove for hours and hours and we didn't stop, then the car ran out and we stuck and now we had to walks and find a place to stay for the night and think what should be next and but we were exhaust and tired and no foods and water, and we didn't wants to drink infect water and turn into a zombies, but Ray was more eager to eat and drink and I did warn him but he didn't wants to listens to me until I pointed out what were happened to him if he drank the water, at that moment he was about to take a drink and then the "zombies" came and I said you were become one of them, and he spill the water and spite out the foods in his mouth.

"Please don't let me become a zombies but I have no control of the matter so we are both risk and whatever happened, it will!

Kelly said to Ray we need to find a shelter before the zombies spotted us. I totally understand, Kelly but I do want to sees my children and my wife again! I do understand Ray, I went home and discover, that they are zombies, at first I thought I were be able to help them but the antibody didn't works and they still were zombies, and the dose was the right amount but it was in the blood. Then Kelly said I thought you were single and I make love with you and about your wife? She probably is a zombies and someone killed her, but I do wants to be with you and I don't wants to died alone and you do looked like my wife with the long blonde hair and the blue eyes and you are about five feet and four inches tall, yes. And a little overweight and I do like your curve, and I do like being with you and this could be our last night and we could end of dead.

"They are getting closer and closer" and I don't wants to be "dead meat". Looked I sees a house and maybe we can stay there for the night, but looked it is evaded by the zombies, then the thunder and lighting occurs and then it rain very heavy and Kelly said we will runs into more zombies because it more acid rain and the dead will come back to lives.

Don't says that Kelly I don't wants to hears that anymore, I just wants to be in a house and being safe, so do I.

"Then Kelly said ok we can go to the barn and we can stay there"!

Are sure about this? Well we have no choice right now so comes with me and so he follow her and later that night, and they make love and then they saw a farmer come inside with a rifle and pointed at them and said get out of here instantly, and Kelly looks at him and he was about to shoot them, and a zombies came in back of him and Kelly tried to warns him but he refuse to listened to her, and then Kelly and Ray tried to help him but he was bitten and dead on the ground and then they saw the white jeep and got Inside and no keys, Kelly and Ray came out into the woods.

Lost and Confuse

Kelly and Ray ran into different direction and Kelly was looking for Ray but she couldn't find him and the same for Ray.

Then Kelly stops and looks around but they were coming toward her and she heard a moaning sound and but was not sure what to do at that moment, but Kelly sidetrack and when back to the barn and spotted Ray and called out and told him to runs toward her.

Then she saw the farmer became the dead and wanted to chew on Ray and somehow Kelly saw a rifle next to her and pick it up and pull the trigger and shout the zombies in the head and Ray ran to her and said thanks for coming back for me, I wouldn't leave you and you do means a lot to me, I feel the same for you. But I don't know which ways to go.

That day we walks in circle and we ended up at the same place and I was really worry we were hungry and thirsty and no place to go and sleep and the zombies were behind us and any minute were been bitten but in some ways we were lucky this time. Somehow we ended up at the river and thought about crossing the bridge, but it was broken.

"We need to cross and sees what on the other side, are you sure about that's "? I think that we should go there and I think we might be safe, don't you think that zombies are not in the water, I don't know but we cannot stay here, fine. But Ray was a bit scare about going on the other side and so was Kelly but she kept quiet. When they cross the bridge they saw the house and Ray said let check it out and sees if there is any foods and water, and Kelly said it can be infection and you will gets the virus, at this point I don't care, then I will have too shoot you in the head, because you will become a zombies., that fine! At least I won't starve.

I will be alone and what will happened to me, I don't wants to lose anymore of my friends do you understand what I am saying? Yes it is clear to me and I won't do anything stupid to end up dying.

Promise me that you will not eat the foods or drink the water from the faucet, but I am thirsty so am I. but we need to test the foods and water first, ok! If it good then we will eat it up and drink alls the water that we wants. Otherwise don't eat it yet! I won't say Ray, they enter the house and lock the door and they got close and then Kelly took out the kit and tested the water and the foods and then she said, "Looks they are out there"! No, I don't believe this. But they are near the doors and we have no escape but are quiet and don't make a sound.

But Ray was a little paranoid and started to walks and screams and loud sound so the zombies were coming more and more and then she knock it out and tied his mouth and his hands and said to her I had no choice, but you are making it more difficult to handle this situation, Ray.

Now the zombies know that we are here and we are trap because of your screaming and loud voice, sure I was in danger before but never in this situation that you put in... Now I need to put the woods over the doors and windows and survive this ordeal, that you place us.

Don't blame me because I was not sure about coming here, but I did follow you and now we will end up being "dead meat' don't says about that, we will make it, you are illusion, no I am.

Meanwhile Ray was tied up and Ray said let me loose and I will behave, promises, no until I think of a plan and then Kelly saw a computer on the desk and said I will try the internet and get some help, do you think that the internet, were it be working, why are you negative about everything?

Come on comes to the real world and get out of the fantasy world I am not. Probably you thought it were be fine, and no one is around but zombies, I know that's! I am not giving up and I will get someone on the internet and we will be safe do you understand said Kelly.

About one hour later, Kelly put on the computer and said so far it is working and I think I will tried to get my friend Brian to contact the military and save us, good plan unless if they are alls zombies, don't says that Ray.

So Ray told Kelly get off the internet and he was about to send a email to Brian, and suddenly fell on the floor and Kelly said what wrong Ray I don't know but I feel weak and I really don't what happened but I will be fine are you sure, but you do like pale, no you are getting the virus and I need to give a shot and you will recover quickly, no I am not getting the virus but I am so hungry and I need the energy and eat some foods and water, alls this time without foods, your body will effective your thinking that is true.

Ok! So Kelly pick him up and then put him on the couch and he sat there and Kelly said I will fry eggs and some toast and I believe the food is not effective and so we can eat, fine. So Kelly when into the kitchen and started to cook the eggs and then Ray came in and he was acting a bit weird and Kelly said Ray what wrong, what he was walking kind of shaking and not straight, and then Kelly saw his face and he was a zombies, and she had to shoot him in the head, but Ray approach her and then fell to the floor and she smash his head and took him to the basement and burn him, and she sat alone in the living room and thought that he probably got bit near the house and she said to herself and I didn't notice that.

Now I am alone and I have no one and Kelly started to cried and said why? Why am I alone, I might be the only, then she saw someone walking in with flames and it was Ray and Kelly said I thought I burn you and you got of the fire and he was about to bite her and then she slam him down and he was dead and once again Kelly carry him to the furnace and burned him. Kelly didn't looked back and then decided to leave the house and go some place else and search for surviving and but first need to finish the email to Brian, and Kelly thought to herself what are the chances that Brian is not a zombies and able to save me, that were be my faith, but I need to send to him immediately, so Kelly send it and just waiting for the reply. Then Kelly kept the internet on and waited and waited and then fell asleep, and about two hours after the nap, then there was a beep and it was a email from Brian., and he answered I am alone in a apartment in Manhattan and I need your help.

Then Kelly reply I was a friend of Ray but he became a zombies and I do need your help, would you comes to me. Then he reply I am trap, and I have no escape, but you have a ways to get me I live near Madison and 125th and I live on the 25 floor, then Kelly reply I don't have a car, and I am miles and miles away from you, we are both trap and I believe that we might not make it, and then he reply, do you have someone in the city that might help me? A moment Kelly didn't says anything but thought of Jim Cook, the chef that work at the restaurant on the green, and now Kelly was thinking of his email and then it pop to her and send too him.

Then she thought to herself that at least someone will get rescue and I would save someone, and I probably would died.

At moment, Kelly heard trucks coming by the house and men with rifles and machine guns and then Kelly steps out and they were about to shoot her and then Larry said don't shoot her and she is not a zombies and they took her into the truck and she told them about Brian, and the captain said we are headed that ways! Do you know where he is located? Yes I do, and she sat in the truck and the zombies were not too bad far from them.

About two hours later they were in Manhattan, New York, there were many and many zombies, they started to shoot and fires there guns and the zombies were falling on the ground and then they saw thousand and thousand of zombies and the captain said we cannot stay here we need to leaves, but we need to find Brian and take him with us.

He might be dead or a zombies, but listens to me we need to find him I promise that I would, we are not going to risk our men because one man, and the lives will be lost don't you understand?

I do but he is not a zombies and he need our help, captain, looked at those body parts and bloods stains in the streets.

They drove toward Madison and then Kelly said this is the building and I we too go upstairs to the 25th floor to rescue him, fine!

They alls when inside and took the elevator and press 25 and they got to the floor and then Kelly knock at the door and then Brian open the door and out of breathe and said to Kelly, you find me, but it is too late.

What do you mean? Looked I am infection and leave me and let me died, no I can give a anti dose, it not going to help me I been infection more than five hours and I am going wants to eat your brain.

Then the captain shot him in his head and said we need to go now and we need go immediately, fine.

They went into the elevator and when down and then into the lobby and then the captain said now we are trap.

"Trapped In Manhattan, New York"

We need to figure out a plan to get out of here and into the truck, we need a distract, do you hears me? Yes and I will do it and it was my fault, yes you will do it and we will try to get you save. Meanwhile a lot shooting and fighting and then somehow they manage to escape but Kelly somehow stay in the lobby and the Captain took a risk and get her out and his name was Lee, and he like Kelly and the others men didn't like what was going on that he was distract and in love with her.

They told him to leave her and him refuse to do so.

At that moment, he steps out of the truck into the sidewalk and walks and knock down the zombies and then Kelly let him in and then they both would inside and then the count of three they step out and gunfire and they were in the truck,. But they were not out of danger; thousand of zombies were coming, and now what? Drive fast and get out of here and that is an order, yes sir.

They drove over the Bronx bridge and headed to the Washington bridge to Atlantic city and drove for hour and hour until they got to Atlantic city and then they got out of the truck and walks and walks to the beach and soak there feet in the sand, and the water, then he grab her and gave her a kiss, and she slap his face. Why did you to do that?

Later that day they make love on the beach and the men were on the watched and they lied on the sand and he was on top of her and then he turn her over and then they lied in each other arms and then they went swimming and then,. One of the men spotted that zombies were in the water and he yelled out and no one heard him and he ran closer and then Lee heard him and then Kelly saw them and they both swam out of the water and got dress and the zombies were coming out of the water and they ran to the truck and drove away.

Do you see them? Yes I see they and they are following us and I think that they might catch us, no kidding an I am totally serious.

But I don't like to me in this situation, I don't neither but this terrible nightmare does not end and I wants everything to be back to normal.

Whoever because this infection and they cannot stop it and the man did start this he is dead, but he did have an anti dose help those who were infection but not totally cure.

But that doesn't help us and we cannot stops and time is running out and the moon eclipse is coming and it will get dark and danger.

Also you have heard about the vampire / zombies they looked like they are not infection but the most danger species around.

Tell me about them, I ran into them and I thought I was a goner but somehow I escape and I can talk about it.

You were the lucky one and my friends became zombies and I had to shoot them in the head, and they wanted to eat my brain.

But that was walking on the beach but then the zombies came and we had to runs and few of your crews got eaten up and then we left New Jersey and headed to Pennsylvania, but I think that is not a such a good idea but I could be wrong, because I came through areas about five month ago and it was thousand and thousand of zombies around and I think I were end of dead, and I hope it won't happened again, I think this time I were be a goner and no one were save me, and even you, Lee.

Why are you saying that's too me? Well alls the time I save the man but never a man save me, that what I am saying.

Lee was driving and saying don't side track and I think I took the wrong turn and I think that we are lost in New jersey and Pennsylvania, and in the woods and a storm coming in, just great! Like we are in a deadly mission and going too died today, shut up. Then the wind and trees falling alls around them and then they saw tunnel coming toward them and they alls jump out of the truck and the truck flew away and then Kelly said that was a close called and but I am glad that I am on the ground not in the sky, but looked behind you a zombies, you must be kidding.

So Kelly whack the zombies in the head and ran up to Lee and said, we safe but not safe enough from the zombies, that is true. So let moving before we do gets bitten and turn into a zombies, you are paranoid, no I am not I saw my friends turn into zombies and I don't wants to lose more friends anymore, do you understand Lee, yes I do.

It is still dark and the rain is falling, the wind is blowing and the trees are falling and the roofs are flying and we have no place to stays and now what we have zombies about a mile away and they are getting closer and I don't know how to stops them.

But we will get away from yes; I promise you will be safe.

Sure at this point I don't know I am going to gets the virus and not turn into a zombies and once again I am going not to died today.

Then Kelly and Lee said I see a house and we can stay there, yes let go and I will follow you… Kelly said I am not too far from you.

Then he turned back and watch out they are taking closer too you runs and don't get caught, I won't be there dead meats.

About a minute later, Kelly and Lee were in the house and also the crew would the look out from the zombies, when they step inside they saw torn bodies and bloods alls over the room, and at that moment, Kelly wanted to vomit and she said I cannot stay here. So where do you wants to go?

Where are no zombies and no death? There is no place like that's!

Kelly walks out and Lee saw a radio to call out for helped, and no one response and Lee said I am not giving up and I am not going too died here.

Then the rain stops and Kelly steps outside and walks around the house and Lee notice that he ran out and said are you nuts, you wants to get infection? No I just want to breathe and relax.

Lee when up to Kelly and kissed her and pull her inside the house and said doesn't do this again! I promise I won't! Later that night: Lee and Kelly decided when something like I become zombies, you shoot me in the head. Yes I will and I will not think about it and I will killed you if you are infection I will do the same too you, do you understand, what I am saying and Kelly said yes I do and I don't wants to talked about it, I just wants make hot passion love too you, me too said Lee.

Later that night, Lee got up and saw the zombies standing near the house and he was worry to tell Kelly that they might not make it and he doesn't want to bring that up at that moment, and then Kelly said what are you thinking well, things were normal and no zombies around, I know I think of the past life and we have nothing to change it but just being alive.

"Every words that you says it is true" yes and I hope that we don't end up being "dead meat" no I will make sure, Kelly, great!

Then they both fell asleep and then Kelly suddenly woke up and heard a noise and check it out and then woke up, Lee and said they are trying to break in and I am scare that they might gets inside and I don't wants to be dead, no I will protection you Kelly and I will protection you Lee.

Then Kelly went to bed and fell asleep and Lee got up and pried open the door and sees where, the zombies were but he was surprise, where they near the door and was about to grab his hand and he called out to Kelly and Kelly ran up and hit the hand of the zombies and pull Lee inside and said are you crazy? No I just wanted too sees where they were.

You are so stupid, and I don't wants too lose anymore of my friends include you, yes I know but we cannot stay here neither.

I will help you and we will make it, I heard that before and it is hard to believe, and I am doing my best.

Lee said we need to leave this place and head south and keeping going that we don't sees anymore zombies, I think that we need to reach local 16 near the border of Florida and Mexico, you got too be serious, that was the last bulletin on the "special report", ok!

But how do we gets there, we are out of gas and I don't want to walks miles and miles to get caught by the zombies.

But we have nom choice but we need to move or we will end up being "dead Meat", thanks for remaining me about that's!

So Kelly and Lee kept on walking and then Lee decided to take a break and said I cannot go any longer and I need to sit here for a while. Do you think it ok too stay here, I think so. Not really sure about anything these days, I am not neither, that great I guess we lost our confidence and probably our life too, don't you ever says that again!

I am not going too died and I am going to survive this ordeal so will you.

I have enough of talking and we need to find the military and gets shot are you crazy, no but we will be safe, probably dead, shot in the head.

No, I don't want to hear this non sense, but this happening now!

Bloods and Body Parts

Lee and Kelly said I know what happening but it is like a nightmare and sees those body parts and bloods and I hope that we don't end up that ways, but we don't know what will occurs in a second and what will happens and who is hiding in the bushes and walks out and bite us or torn us a part, I don't wants to hears that Lee, I just wants to be home.

Well you should realize that home is not home anymore, but I can think it could be again! I think it happening again and I don't wants to died and I wants to lives and have a family and be happy, it will happened? But when the military killed alls the zombies and then it will be normal, so how will the military know that we are not infection and we probably end up dead, don't says that Lee, I don't wants to hears that's! You are very sensitive about surviving the virus and you really did! But this is my first and I loss a lot of my friends, so did I, and they are the "walking dead" I know.

But looked Lee, the body parts and alls the bloods on the street and they can be coming out and eaten us up and we will be dead, stop that's! Either we gets shot in the head by the military or being dead meat for the zombies, so what are the odd about that's! I don't know but stop talking about it and just keeps on moving, fine!

"Soon it will be getting dark and we need to find a shelter to stay for the night and so far I don't see anything yet! But we will, so why are you so positive when it is so bad out here? I don't know.

That night they kept on walking up a road and suddenly the zombies were in front of them and in back of them and how what?

Looked said to Lee, run into the path and I think that we will be safe, and you think so? Yes I do, so Kelly and Lee ran up and then Kelly said I see a red barn and we should go there! Ok! So they ran up to the barn and Lee looked inside and said it is clear and we can lock up and we will safe.

But not totally, but a little safe for now, and Kelly said look here is a gun and we can shoot them zombies in the head,, and Lee look at the gun but no bullets and that is just great, then they heard a sound in the barn and it was the farmer, and it was a zombies that wanted to bite my arm and I took a stick and poke it into his head.

Then they saws more zombies coming toward Lee and Karen, and now what we are trap and Lee said climb up and jump out of the window, I am not leaving you behind.

So now and Kelly said no I am staying, you will get killed if you stay but you will too so they try to figure out what to do and then Lee took a pitch fork and poke to the zombies lies on the floor and a second later, one other zombie grab Kelly leg and drag her down and Lee came and poke the zombie in the head with pitch fork.

Kelly said more are coming and we need to get out of here immediately, I hear you what you are saying. Ok I won't disagree with you and I will take your advice, thanks! Stop talking and we need to go now and no stalling, ok we need go now. Yes I am coming, and then she took the gun with the bullet, and Lee said why did you take the gun? Maybe we will find some bullets and shoot the zombies. Ok! But you are not sure what you saying but I have a bad feeling being here so do I so let go and talking and find a house that we can stay for longer than one night, so where is that Place? I don't have a clue, what I am doing and I also don't wants to be dead meat for the zombies either, I don't want that's!

Now Lee and Kelly walks and walks and the zombies were not too far from Lee and Kelly so, Kelly said I will fight to lives, me too!

Just talking about it, does not help so we need too get weapons and bullets and not zombies, I do agree, but you know that the virus is spreading like wild fires, yes I do and we can be infection and it can be airborne, you could be right, but I hope not!

Lee and Kelly walks and walks once again and they saw a mansion and water near by and Kelly said let go there, are you sure? Yes I am starving and wants to gets a bath and Lee said maybe we can have some fun and being together, and Kelly said "you wants sex now" when we are being hunted by zombies, well this could be our last night together, that true, but you need to watch the house if the zombies approach when I take the bubble bath and then a nap, so can you that for me?

Sure I can do that for you but don't fall asleep, you must be kidding me.

"Meanwhile Kelly when upstairs and put on the water and looked out and it was a sunny July day and then Kelly took off her clothes and the water was running and then the bubble in the bath, then Kelly step inside the tub and then lay in the tub and put a towel and close her eyes.

About one hour later, Kelly was still fast asleep and meanwhile Lee, suddenly fell asleep and then suddenly the door open and about a minute later about twenty zombies were in the house and they surround Lee, and then he suddenly woke up and he was about to get bitten, but Lee had a butcher knife in his hands, and stab the zombie in the head.

But meanwhile Kelly was still sleeping and didn't hears anything then she woke up and heard Lee screaming and saying Kelly I need your help hurried, the zombies are inside and then Kelly came out of the bath and got dressed up in a hurried ran down with a letter opener and about that moment Kelly thought that Lee was about to get bitten, and she stab the zombie in the head and kick one with her leg and Lee was still on the floor and then Kelly pull him up and looked at him but didn't says a word.

About one hour later, Kelly said I thought you were watching the door but you fell a sleep and we could have ended up dead. And Lee tried to apologize and I don't want to hear the apology!

Fine, I just messed up big time, I am only human, I know that's!

But I think we should leave, I don't think, I will lock this place started with the doors and windows and we should be fine! Ok! Well you should start doing that now and we will stay here for awhile until the military comes and rescue us and we can be together and be happy, I don't even that that word in my mind right now, so slow down and keep us safe until helps arrival, sure, I will.

It was about midnight after the attack and Kelly and Lee were on there guard and make sure that were not happened again!

But Lee was not totally sure if they were be safe or not but he was very silent , and Kelly looked out of the window, and said well I think they are gone, I hope so because we don't have any weapons to fight with and I don't know if we are going to make it too morning, don't says that is very negative, fine and he walks away from Kelly and looked outside and he notice something but was not sure that moment, than he saw more zombies heading there ways and told Kelly, just great! Now what I don't know but we need to be quiet and turn off the lights, are you crazy? No I am not, if you were alone you probably end dead, thanks a lot! You think that I am weak but I am much stronger than you, no ways you are a lady and you being stronger that is a joke, no it is not I save you how many times? So you are counting? No but it seem, like you are? No I am not!

Then Lee walks away from Kelly and when into the other room and sat down and Kelly said what are you doing? I am taking a break.

Fine, so I will lookout and sees if they are coming too the house, fine!

Five hour later that night, the storm came in and it was pitch black and it was never before. and on the "special report" said that the government was going to send out nuclear missiles to killed the undead and Kelly said we are going to died from the nuclear blast and we will be goner! No we are going to hide in the shelter and we will not be infection.

But are you sure about that's yes I am and we are going there now, and we have one hour too get there! But it is pitch black and we will be caught by the zombies, no we wills not follows where I go and you go!

Then the rain came down and the undead came to lives, and Kelly said there are about a thousand blocking the door, and we have no escape plan. No we don't but don't worry we won't get infection or be eaten up zombies, well you promises too much and I don't if you will be able to keep your promise, I will you will sees.

The rain pour so heavy and Kelly was looking out and they were coming out of the graves and Lee said I probably chose the wrong place to be safe, but I didn't know this was part of the cemetery, it was dark and I thought this was a mansion but I was wrong this is grave house.

No I don't believe that! That is true, I cannot believe that you brought me here, and Lee said I am sorry about this but I will gets us out of here!

Now there were mores than 5 thousand zombies near the house and then they heard a crackling sound and it was a zombies climbing out of the coffin, and he was about to bite me, so I push him away and I ran for my life through the graveyard. That moment, the rain was hard, I could see!

"They are going to get you" Kelly!

Kelly ran to the car but the doors were locked and Kelly struggle and could not open the door, somehow Lee was in back of her and gave her the keys and about a minute later, Lee was about to get caught by the zombies, Kelly pull him inside the car and drove away.

Then Kelly said we don't have too much gas and it might last about a mile or unless, you must be kidding me? Nope I am totally serious what going on here, so do have a solution, we maybe we should to go Maine?

Lee said but we cannot because we don't have the gas and the nuclear blast will soon comes here and we will be goner, I don't wants to hears anymore negative from you Lee, there must be more survivors out there?

You could be right but I don't think that we are going to find them, but then Lee came out with the line (They are going to get you) Kelly! Stop that I don't like what you are saying, I survive the first batch of zombies and I will survive these zombies do you understand you are getting on my nerve, fine! Later that night they drove about a mile away and the car stall and they got out of the car and walk the rest of the ways to town, and it was in the countryside, and no sound of any kinds at alls.

Lee said I don't really like it here but we have no choice about staying here until help comes, Kelly said. No we will looked around and check out the café and then if it is ok we will stay for two hours and then move something else. Maybe we should stay the night, let rest for a while and take a snooze. Meanwhile Kelly fell asleep and Lee got up looked around and when outside the café and walks the street and then he saw the zombies coming toward him, and he ran inside and woke up Kelly, we cannot stay, but why? Because the zombies are here and we are trap and I don't know how we are going to leaves here.

I told you this was a bad idea to be here but you didn't listen to me! But don't nagged me, I won't! Honey and walks away and went because the counter and took a piece pie. Lee said don't eat the pie, said to Kelly.

You think that I will get infection but I don't think so I don't think it not in the food, and then Kelly said I find a radio, let listen to it and maybe they have a update what is going on in the world., that true we are someplace unknown and probably going to get shot in the head because they will think that we are zombies, no don't says that Lee. I have heard story that undead are not the only that are getting killed off; stop saying that I don't wants to listen to your nonsense, ok!

Lee said I won't says anything stupid like that again; good I don't wants to hit you on the face. For what why are you acting like a bitch? No I am not! Kelly walks away and Lee follow her and said I am sorry Kelly for saying that's! Ok! I forgive you, but you were talking about Maine.

Yes I think that place is not infection in Maine and we need to get there immediately, sure but how? Walks, and find a car with gas, easy said then done, sure! But why can we wait until morning to start walking and the storm is still here and I think we should stay, so make up your mind, ok!

So where do we sleep, I think that we should sleep on the floor and lock the door and windows, and about a minute later they heard a knock and they thought it was a zombie, but it was a young girl, and Kelly said Let her in, are you crazy? No, I am not! So Kelly said unlock the door and let her in, are you taking a chance of getting infection by letting her in? Yes she is a child and I think she need our help, fine, so Lee unlock the door and behind her was her parents and brother, and her brother was like he was sick with the parents, and Kelly said come on in. then Lee notice that her brother had a mark on his hand and the girl said we were on the ways to New York and we came up some kind of creatures, well they are called zombies, oh I didn't know that's! Then Lee asked there names and the girl said Crystal, and my brother name is Mars and my parent's names and Venus and Pluto, you must be joking no mister.

So where are you from, well we are from original from Oregon, and you far from home yes, our relatives became zombies, and they wanted us for a meal. Oh I see! Crystal but how did you get here, well we flew on a jet and got here! But who flew you here? My uncle that turned into a zombies and our plane crash and we somehow didn't get killed in the process. Now we want to go to New York City to my cousins and they are probably alive, I don't think so! The city is infections and thousand and thousand of zombies are there! We just came back from there! The whole family came inside and sat and then the sick lies down and throwing up and Lee said they are sick and they will become zombies.

But Crystal will not let us killed them when they become zombies, she will fight us so I have a plan to tied her up and then we will killed her family that are sick, fine! But I don't wants any part of killing do you understand?

So Kelly took Crystal to the other room and Crystal said I know what you are doing? So what am I doing said Kelly to Crystal? Well I know that your friend will killed my family because they are sick and they will become zombies. I know that I don't want to leave them I wants to, be there when your friend killed them, and I wants to remember how they were not how they are now. I do understand what you are saying but you are too young to watched, no I am not!!

They both walks back into that room and Lee was pointed a knife toward the head and Crystal ran up to her parents and brother and about that moment she was about to gets bitten and Lee ran very quickly to her and pull her arms away and he was slight cut and blood was dripping from his arms and Kelly then scream out and said it is alls my fault that you are hurt. You better believe it, you got me infection and you will not have a chance of living without me, and then Kelly said, looks you are not infection and so stab that bastard and whore with the knife into the head.

Lee pushed Crystal on the floor, where her brother lies and then he saw that she was going too died. Somehow Lee ran out and pick her up and said to Kelly I am so sorry to you got you into this situation, but you were not the one let them in but I did and it is my fault and I don't wants to talked about it and just leave and get away from here and forget.

But it is impossible, because we are trapped and also we have some zombies inside and when they wake up they will eat us up.

Soon the morning will comes and we will be able to travel safe because I believe we won't become zombies, and we won't get the infection neither ok, and Crystal spoke I thought you were help me but you killed the ones that I loved and I am alone, no you are not we will take you with us to the where we can walks the streets and no zombies, so where is that place exactly,, said Crystal someplace in Maine and we will go there in the morning, well if my parents don't eat us up, and then Crystal I cannot leave them, I am not going I decided to stay here,, and Kelly said are you crazy? No, I loved my family and I will die with them. No you are too young too died, well my brother is dead and he is a year younger than I.

I think we should go to sleep now and we will see the morning and we will decide but I make my own decision about staying and you cannot change my mind, Kelly, fine! Meanwhile Lee was on the watched and said, I probably can go to sleep and this place is locked up good so I think that I am going too bed and he lies next to Kelly. And he put his arms around her and about one hour later, Kelly heard a sound and woke up and it was Crystal parents over them and Kelly kick them on the floor and Lee woke up and started to fight with them, and Crystal got up and when in front of her family and they grab her and bite her in the arms and it started to bleed. And Kelly tried to rescue her but almost got caught and Lee pull her and stab them in the head and then the brother got up and was about to Pull Lee and Kelly step in and stab him in the head and a moment Lee, Crystal became a Zombie.

Lee and Kelly took a knife and stab her and she fell to the ground and then they heard a bang and then the zombies got inside and Kelly and Lee ran out but they were being chase. Kelly said to Lee, I think that I left the map to Maine and I need to go back and get it. So Kelly and Lee went back to the café and then they approach the door and Crystal was standing there! Kelly said I thought we killed her. We did, I guess not an enough that she got up, that true and once again they stab her and she dies. Then Kelly said I find the map and now we can go are you sure yes I am. They steps out and walks into the street and suddenly helicopters were flying over there head and explosions, and fire burning and Kelly said they are killing off the zombies and we are in the middle of it and you are right! Hope that we won't get killed, just keeping running and tried not too gets hit and so I will do that Lee. When got down the street there was a military truck and they were unable to leave.

Strict Area

This is a strict areas and you are not allow to comes in, you may be infection and we need to test you before you are allow to come into this section and I need to speak to my general and then Kelly said sir if you won't let us in we will get into infection and then somehow he recognize Kelly and said was your dad was in the service? Yes he was the colonel but I still cannot make the rules and regulation, I do understand sir.

Meanwhile they sat near the gate and the zombies and the time was ticking and Kelly knew that they need to be on the other side and I do have a plan. So what is the plan well I need to sneak inside and check out the computer and sees if we can find out what going on!

Ok, you need to watch out when I go into the tent and I will go online and sees where a safe place to go is! But don't get caught, shut up.

Meanwhile Lee was distract the solider and Kelly snuck inside and then when online and she notice that the US government did test and it just went wrong and they had antidote but not enough for the whole population, so some persons will not be sure to dies.

Lee was talking back and forward and but the soldier just didn't want to listen what he was saying and he was about to leave his post and go into the tent and check on the computer and meanwhile Kelly print the information and turn off the computer and started to walks out and then Lee make a scene and Kelly snuck out under the fence and ran back to Lee. Then the soldier left and Kelly said comes to me I need to show you something, so what is it? Government is behind this endemic, and we are going to dies if we don't stop it, do you understand? Yes but how do we gets across and tell other humans that they are test lab experience.

But I don't know how many are alive or they probably are zombies.

Don't say that Kelly I just want to have my life and career and be happy again, so do I and my family too.

But Lee you need to be quiet and don't says a word to the solider because he will betray us and maybe even taking to the lab and make us sick, and Kelly and Lee agree that they will keeps there mouth shut. About ten minutes later, Kelly said to Lee don't you hears them, what? The zombies are getting closer and we are in the open and I think that we should go the wood and hide there, because the zombies will attack the base and I don't want to be in the middle of the chaos. I totally understand and let go and the solider said where are you going? We are tried and we are going to rest and we will be back soon! The solider walks away and about half hour later, the zombies came to the gate and ate the solider and blood and parts then there were shooting and fire gun heard in the woods, and Lee said how you knew, it happened six month ago in San Diego base and I was almost dead.

So I don't want to stick around and be dead meat so move it and we will find a place to stay and I think there is a bridge but shelter from inside that no one were sees us. And we were being safe.

So far that I listens to you I am still alive and not dead and you really know what you are doing, sure this is not my first you know and it won't be my last neither, I got your message. Good! But please be silent and don't make a sound they will hears us and the smell that we are alive they will hunted us and we will be dead, I know I will.

It got really dark and they didn't even put on a candle or flashlight because the zombies would find them if they did. Do you hear anything; no I have not, so far that we are ok but for how long I don't know...

They both kept quiet and the noise was getting louder and Kelly said to Lee I think that we should leave now but why? They are not too far from us. They both started to leaves but they were block on both sides and Kelly thought to herself now we need to find a hole and get out of here immediately do you understand? Yes I do, I am looking in the woods in the bridge so far I cannot find one so we are trap but not long. Are you sure about that? But time is ticking and the zombies are very near and they will catch us we are only on a wooden bridge and it is not locked so it is open and they can jump stomp in and eat us up and we would be dead that is totally true and I cannot disagree with you so we need to be ready to runs, and not looking back, yes I know the routine, did it many times before. Yes, yes I do know understand what your saying and they are coming I don't know which direction they are coming from but it somehow we separate, I will find you do understand, yes! No hesitate about where I am just keeps on running! Fine, stop talking start running, I will be behind you, that is good to hears and I will not be frighten, sure I when through this before and this is not the first time in my life dealing with the zombies and I don't know how long it will last. One thing I do wants to survive this ordeal and have a family and have a career in writing and so about Lee, well my dream is being on a talk radio and having children and living in Beverly Hills and ground pool and being with friends. That is a nice dream and it will happen, do you believe that?

I do, and you should too, I am trying very hard and but sometime it is so hard to think what will be back to normal and when we can just relax and have fun and not worry about the undead coming too lives.

Will it happen? I cannot answer that's! because we don't know if we are going make it in five minutes when the undead comes here and will be get out of here, that is true but I don't have no doubt about that Lee. We do need to continue and not give up and fight for ours lives, yes I know. Later that day, Lee said I will take a peek out there, are sure you will be safe to looked around and don't be long I won't I will be back in five.

Meanwhile Kelly sat on the bridge and tries to use her cell phone but there was no service and just sat there and then she heard that Lee was yelling and said get out of there now! They are coming!!! Kelly got up and which entrance do I use on the front or the back, but then Kelly saw them coming toward her and she ran out into Lee arms and kissed him, but he was acting not the same has before but he had changed. Lee looked at her like she was his meal and Kelly kind of broke away from him and ran into the woods and then he followed her in the woods. Now Kelly was worried that she will be a zombie soon and her best friend was doing it to her. No, Lee what are you doing don't you remember me?

Lee looked at her and smiles but then she saw his mouth and it was bloody and infection and then Kelly said did you have some water from the bottle that called clear blue water? He nodded his head and Kelly said why did you do that's I have warns you and somehow you didn't listen to me, but why? We came so far and now I need to kill you and I will be alone. Lee came up to her and said sorry but you need to go now and don't looked back and just keep going toward the Maine border and you will be safe, that my word. I will but I need to shoot you first, well I do it myself, just go Kelly, and Lee kissed her goodbye and Kelly left and kept on walking and crying alls the ways to Maine. About half hour Kelly heard a shot and

Lee fell down to the ground and he was dead. Kelly was turning around and thinking what a wonderful man that Lee was too her and would never forget him, and Kelly stop for a moment and thought, I am starving and hungry and what will I eat and drink and I don't wants to be infection, sat for while and then got up and walks again and now she was reaching the border of Maine and Kelly didn't know what was in that state and what will happened to her, but kept on walking and she was near the town and it was nice and she saw children playing in the street and peoples walking around and well thought to be normal and she step into the diner and sat down and order bacon and easy over eggs and coffee, and sat there, and then the foods was serve and then Kelly still looking around and was about to eat and a man walks inside and he was bloody and dirty hands and then Kelly looked around once again! Kelly got up and said I need too use the restroom and the waitress pointed to the door and Kelly when inside and then saw the window and snuck out and thought to herself that if she ate the foods they were been infection.

About a minute later the waitress was looking for Kelly and said missy where are you going? No place but why are you trying to sneak out of the window. Well, ok I was trying not too eat because of the virus that is spreading from west coast to east coast and I am just afraid to eat,, well honey you just wanted me to get stiff with the check and then my boss would fire me, no madam, I did leave some money on the table but honey you need to eat, and you are saying that there are the undead coming back too lives yes I am? I have not heard that nonsense but come back have some food and don't starve self to death. Well you are not listening too me what I am saying? Not true, what you are saying!

"Walking Dead"

You are saying the dead are coming back to lives? Yes and the waitress you must be kidding me, are you telling me a practical joke? No I am totally serious and I don't wants to eat, so far did not hit the Maine coast and I think I will starve a little more, Kelly, no you cannot and I will give you your eggs and bacon and eat some, ok Beatrice.

So Kelly told Beatrice what was going on with undead walking and Beatrice was surprise to hears about that's! Tell me more Kelly. Ok I will but it is not good and I think it in the water and some foods that we eat, so you don't know what foods that killed you and then you turned into the zombies? That is right but if you don't eat your going died too, but I won't turn into zombies but they will eat you up that is true... I want to know more and what are the warning signs, well the moods changes and then there are how you looked into there eyes that change like that man that walks inside here about half hour ago, oh he is not infection he was born that ways! He was born in LA, ten years ago and his parents would killed in a freaking accident and he came to live with is Aunt Jen, and she take care of him and so that the sorry about that man Roy.

So tell me more, are the peoples of Maine are sick, and are the undead walking the streets? No one is sick or infection, that is good news and I think did not reach this coast yet! But you need to be careful what was going in different states, do you understand?

Ok I will eat the foods and I will stay here for while and I think you should here and you will be safe, I will be I need to find a hotel to stay and take a shower, well down the street and it called crystal ball motel and it is not too expensive, well I just need to rest and sleep for awhile, sure I do.

That day Kelly ate some foods and walks to the motel and check in and Kelly was in room 209 and Kelly put a sign do not disturb, and when into the shower and then to bed, and meanwhile the storm came in with lighting and thunder and the earth shook the ground and then about five hours later, in that town peoples started to feel sick and they when into the emergency room and sirens when off and building burning and moaning and screams in the street, and the virus arrive in Maine with the wicked storm. Meanwhile Kelly was fast asleep and the virus was spreading like wild fires, and about two hours later, Kelly woke up and got up and when to bathroom and then she heard some noise in the lobby and now Kelly knew something was going on!

So Kelly got dressed up and when downstairs and it was not the same.

Now she was wandering if the virus spread there, soon has she thought of that, Kelly looked out of the window and the nightmare begins again!

Kelly thought to herself she cannot stay there anymore and need to find a safe place, and then once again she looked out and it was Roy and he was one of the zombie, oh my god! What will I do? I need to get away now. So Kelly got her thing and walk out of the room and looked around and then thought I need a weapon, but where can I find one, and then suddenly Kelly got a stomach ache and said no, I cannot be infection and then she pull out the antidote and gave herself a shot and sat for awhile and got up left the room and walk out and saw the chaos in the street and spotted a van and ran into blue and gray van and started up and drove away and then she saw Beatrice and called out to her and but she didn't hears her and then stop the van and once again called out and then Beatrice looked at her and said go now save yourself and Kelly said no I wants to help you, and Beatrice said it is too late for me and I am infection, no my friend I can help you, I can give you a antidote.

I will not leaves my family and friend and you need to go now and don't looked back and then a man jump into the van and his name was Marco and said, honey you won't be alone and somehow she kick out of her van and drove away crying, and said I don't know where too go now!

But she didn't know that she was not alone in the van and about two hours later, he woke up and he woke up and Kelly at that moment he came into the front and she skidding the van and almost when off the cliff and stop and who are you? My name is Marco and you took my van what? Well you left the keys in the van and I needed to gets way so I took it so maybe I should, called the police. So on called them you probably won't reach them, so you are smart no I went with this ordeal in LA many years ago, and it is spreading, and no one can stop it and what else? I don't understand what you are saying? Just keeping on driving and maybe we can go to New Hampshire and I think that mountain are clear, unless the storm comes in and then the peoples turn into zombies.

So that what happened, Yep! And then there is no cure so far but I do have one antidote left so are you going to give too me?

The antidote doesn't work on everyone and I don't wants to waste it, so you think that I am not worth it? No I don't know if you have the virus? Fine I am worried about anything like that's I believe that I am fine.

Well did you go out in the rain? No I was sleeping in the van. Well you are fine and so you are right and so we need to keeps on going and then stay in a house and peaceful place so we are about one mile to our destination, great! I cannot wait to sees Peoples again! Yes, I agree with you Marco, then I will take a hot shower and a warm bed and so we need to ask for two separate room and that is so awesome!

I cannot wait and I wants to talk with you more Marco and I want too get to know you better, that great and then about a minute later they park the van and when inside and went inside and looked around for the desk clerk and then Tina came out and said can I help you?

Yes we need two room and to stay the night? Well I only one room with two bed is that ok? Kelly looks at Marco ands said ok!

Marco smiles and said don't worry I won't make any advance toward you well why are you insult me? I am trying not too. Sorry Kelly I just like you very much but you don't know you. Don't worry your pretty head about it ok, I won't! Then they went into the room and Kelly took the bath towel and when to take a shower. And Meanwhile Marco try to reach his friend on the cell and but couldn't reach him. Once again he tries and tries again but no luck reaching his friend, and started to talk with Kelly but she said what? I don't hear you what are you saying?

I believe that they will invaded this place too, what I don't know what yours saying, then the special report came on and said come on Kelly you have to hears this, one moment let me gets dressed you wills miss the president conference about the zombies and what to do? Ok I will be there in a second, and Kelly walks in and the President said we are going to fire the missiles in the east coast to contend the endemic of virus and will not spread, and please go into shelter and stay there until the air is clear from the nuclear missiles. You will be hit with a lot chemical and gas and you need to find gas mask and a very close shelter to be not infection with the missile active radar two miles of the Atlantic Ocean near Florida and Mexico Border and also bay by Maine, the sirens will go off in ten minutes from now.. Take shelter and protection yourself.

Do you hear what they are saying? Yes I am and I think that we should leave now and find the shelter now, I agree, said Marco. So I will grab my bags and leave and it was nice staying here for a while but they said near Maine and we are in New Hampshire , but maybe we won't be infection and you willing to take a chance not really so let move your ass, said Kelly to Marco,, and so they got into the van and about two minute later they saw the sky blow up and the earth shook and it was a lot smoke and I cannot sees anything and I think we should stop here, no ways I am going to keeps on going and then Marco said we can end off a cliff and dies. So what is that sound? Sound likes a lot of peoples talking and walking beside us and I don't see anything, it must be in your mind. Fine you don't believe me? I do but I don't sees them or hear them. They kept on going and until the road was clear and then Kelly said, now I see them and I don't know if we can gets away from here... but they are getting very closer to us and I think that we will grab us if we don't drive a little faster.

I am not going to speed, oh you think that you will gets a ticket I don't think unless the zombies is a cop, so don't be so a wise guy and telling me what to do and I don't like that's do understand?

Right now they were shout back and forward and then Marco called her a bitch and she called him a bastard and slap his face and they didn't talk for awhile... then Kelly said I am trying to keeps us alive and you are screwing with my head and I just want to focus where I am driving and I don't wants to miss the exit and then find a location. But at that moment I knew that we were near the destination that we suppose to be. But Marco said but I don't sees anyone that would help us so I think that we should keeps on driving, sure I will until I run out of gas that will be pretty soon and then we will probably be dead meat for the zombies. No, no I don't wants to hears, that we will dies, no more this negative from you Marco and I will kick you out of the van and you will fight for your life with the zombies and I will not comes back for you, I don't like you threaten me like that you pretty girl, and Kelly looked back and it was Crystal in the back seat and drool and strange looks in her eyes. Then Kelly took the stick and stabs her in the head and she fell and Marco dumped on the road. That night Marco and Kelly didn't speak what happened and they knew that they would run into zombies and killed them and then they heard helicopter and tanks, and shooting and seeing body parts and bloody roads. I cannot do this anymore I need help and we are alls alone do to this battle and I cannot do it myself Marco, so would you please help me? Ok!, Ok I will so how can I help you that I don't even know how to fight, and you lady you got gut and you are not afraid of those zombies. No I am and I am not giving up and Kelly kept on driving and then they were shooting at Kelly and the Military think that I am a zombies that is driving a van and they wants to target us and we can end being killed at this point, but you must get across and tell them that we are not zombies but we are alive human being, but they think that we are and I cannot change there mind. You better tell them that we are not zombies. They drove and drove and they were shooting at them and they got hit and they step out of the van and the soldier looked into there eyes and was about too shoot them and then the captain came ands said we been looking for you missy, but why because you have the antidote and you need that right now missy, well my name is not missy, sir and it is Kelly.

They took them pointed a rifle and saying go into the tent and I wants to talk with you it is very important and vital information about the lab that you work near the LAX and how many persons got infection and why are you so special that you don't have the virus, well I think I just didn't use what they were drinking and I so I watched and what occurs that day.

So you are saying that it is in the water and the foods that we eat, sure but it could be, well if I drink the glass of water from the faucet. will I get sick, not sure, sir. So what are you sure and how you kept yourself alive and not killed by the zombies? Not exactly sure but I just knew what to do, well you are really clever. Thanks, so can I leave with my friends no you cannot you are going to be testing and sees if you have the virus, no Kelly walks out and said we are leaving now and she somehow got the gun and pointed and said let us go and we will not says anything to anybodies. You must be kidding me that I will let you go so I guess I will blow your head off and I will leave do you understand, and he called out the guard and said locked them in the cell and don't let them out, you are doing a mistake and you will be sorry and Marco said you better let us go!!! Ok!

"Earthquake"

They were about to leave the base and suddenly the earth shook and Kelly said it must been a atomic bomb and Marco said no it was a tremble and it was a big one, and we cannot stay, and we need to go before the second quake hit, do you understand what I am saying too you Marco, we are not safe and the tremble and earth shook and more the undead will comes back to lives. So they headed back to the van and drove off toward west east on the highway and headed to Vermont, and Kelly said the higher ground and better we will be, seem like you know what you are doing, thanks! So we need to get off the radar and just keeps going on the back road of Vermont and we will be fine and no one will find us and I do have a friend that has a place that we can stay.

So how far he does him live and when will we get there? You asked too many question and just be quiet and let me think. Fine I will be quiet but I was trying to help you, shut up. About a minute later and I do remember and we are going there and he lives really high near the mountain and we will need a snowmobile to get to him, so where do we find one and how far and I told about five miles west and then I need to take a left near the mountain and then go straight and now I know where I am going and we will be there about in one hour time and we will Scott free from the zombies, yes and then we can sleep in a nice bed.

"Marco said that sound good and I cannot wait to get there if some reason that they won't let us in like the military so what do we do? I will figure out a plan to get inside and we will be fine and you worry too much, I know I do. Soon we will reach mountain road and it will lead us to my friend house and we can rest and have foods and not worry anymore, are you positive that the zombies, won't be there!

About half hour we will be there and we need to cross that bridge to go over to the mountain, but we cannot go by car, and need to find a snowmobile and ride up that way, and otherwise we will skid and even have accident. But we will be fine and I know there is a rental place and that we can rent a snowmobile and drive up and it is two blocks down and a left and I remember that place. Do you think that we will run into zombies, I don't think so but in case keeps your eyes open and don't hurry to enter a place quick and why because zombies may bite you, thanks for the warning! Kelly step inside the store and called out his name, Peter, where are you we need your services, and he came out a bit a weird walks and his speak was like he was drunk and I couldn't understand what he was saying, and I said we need to rent a snowmobile to Tony place do you have any available for rent and he nodded his head and said no I don't have anymore today, so you need to comes back tomorrow, fine and Kelly we cannot stay here but we need to go back to the car and then Marco said we are going to freeze. I will put on the put on the heater and stay, inside, I am not going back to the van and I wants to find a motel and stay there and but do you sees one and he answered no I didn't sees. So we will stay a while, but fine and then we will go up to his place and do you think that your friend is not a zombie.

"The Next morning they got up and they didn't realize that they slept in the car and Marco was very close to Kelly and at that moment he gave her a kiss and said I wanted to give you the kiss when I met you, and why didn't you? I was not sure how you like me or not? Then they talk and talk and then Kelly said; now it is time that we go back to the rental and meet up to my friend Tony, that is right! So let go now… they walks very slowly and snow was on the ground and at that moment Kelly fell into the snow and Marco pick her up and said thanks! Then Marco took Kelly hand and they walk hands and hands. Before they when inside, Marco kissed her lips and told her, that he were never leave her. She smiles and said don't says what you don't means. But you means something too me and I don't wants to let you go! Fine but we are wasting time and I just want to go and find my friend and talk to him about what is going on in the world. Does he listen to the news? I don't know but I think he must know what going on and maybe he left his house and went hunting and hope not turned into zombie. So why don't you called Tony and tell him that we are on our ways there, well I don't have his cell number and so I wants to surprise him and I know that he will be happy to sees me. Kelly called and said Peter where are you and then Kelly saw that the floor was with a lot of blood stains and Kelly said we need to leave now, and he said why? Five minute later, he came out and not walking straight and his mouth was filled with blood and drool and Kelly knew that he became a zombie and more are probably around. How do you know that? They started to run and run and then a snowmobile came by and then Kelly called out his name and it was her friend Tony. Tony stops and said what are you doing in New Hampshire, well looking for you my friend and I guess you find me and so he said " did you hears about virus" ? yes that why I came and to see if you knew and so I do and that why I am leaving this terrible place and Kelly said there is no place safe, do you know that's? Nope.

But why are you standing around I will give you a lift from this place and about my friend and he cannot just stay he need to comes with us. I do understand but the seat is only for two persons and not three, so I will come back and take your friend, I promise you so take the seat, fine. So Kelly and Tony left Marco in the open and no shelter and they drove to the car and Kelly said "remember to pick up my friend and I will"!

At that moment, the earth shook and Marco fell down the mountain and Kelly had to hold on to Tony and she said don't let me go I won't! You need to get Marco now but I cannot not at this moment, we just had an earthquake and the road is crack, and then fine I will get him myself. No you are not going I am you do think you are? Well an old friend from high school that we once dating for awhile. That is true, but stop talking about the past and we need to stick with the present, I agree with you. Later that day Kelly and Tony to search for Marco and they when back to the rental place and he was not there and now what? I don't have a clue what to do? Please help me out Tony, and Marco is a close friend of mine and I need to find him, sure I will help you so I will get a flashlight and we will search and once again the earth shook and Kelly fell into Tony arms and he held her and kissed her very gentle with his lips. Wait a minute you just kissed me and you make a pass at me and then Tony said I cannot stop thinking of you so I had to kiss you, but why I did you? You were here and so was I, that why I kiss you and you kiss me back and then they heard Marco screaming for help. Then Tony climb down and Kelly had a rope in her hand and hold it tight to keep Tony tied and try to reach Marco and it took a while and now Kelly was getting worry if the zombies were going to get them and now she was yelling and screaming and said hurry it going to be dark soon. When Tony reaches Marco and he wounded and bleeding from the mouth and he was weak and Tony said we will need to call someone for the rescue because I am not able to carry him myself. Can I help so you want to be stuck with us and then what will do, then? I don't know but standing here, like a target. Sure if you want to help come down and be with us, sure I am coming down and when she said that some zombies were coming closer to her and Kelly just decided to jump on to the rope and Tony caught and then pull the rope down and now we will have to climb the mountain down, instead of going up and Kelly I know that you been train in that field, sure that was a long time ago, and I remember don't remember how I did it. Kelly looked up the zombies seems like they were going to comes down and Kelly said we need to go now and go on the next level and be safer there, are you sure, Kelly,, why don't we just go inside the cave. I guess to hide out and stop the bleeding, sure. But Kelly had a bad feeling about the whole thing going into the cave to hide out from the zombies. Then she thought and thought about the decision Kelly make was it the right one and Kelly was not sure at that moment. Later that night Kelly and Tony check on Marco but he was not in such a good condition and he really needed a doctor and some surgery done but out in the wildness there are no hospital and doctor around to help Marco and he probably might make it, but no one know what will happened to them in the wildness, and the unknown situation, without a radio and a cell with a signal. How we will know what going on in this world we don't have the communication to the outside world what will happened to us? We will be fine and soon we will be leaving here and back to our family, you are right and I cannot wait to sees my sister and mom, and my daughter, Caroline, my daughter is ten year old. I will see her soon, I know I will.

I will hold in my arms and I won't let her go, never again said Marco.

"Rescue"

Do you hears that's? What do you means, like someone is near by? Then someone called out into the cave and said we are the rescue team and we heard your signal for help and came and the epidemic, and you folk will be check out and then send back home to your family, and Kelly said about the virus and it is contain and not spreading, that great and he said follow me and I will take you too the copter and we will be headed to New York city and it alls clear and back to normal after the blast that destroy the virus and Kelly said I need to get back to LA, so that will take a bit while but it is under control too. Kelly smiled to Marco and Tony and said well, you guys I am glad that we would together and hope that we can have reunion and I really would like that's! But Kelly didn't know that Marco was infection and he was being sent to the lab and getting some antidote and more testing and Kelly said sir can I go with my friend Marco? Not right now but we will send you a message or called you about your friend, fine but I would feel better if I when with him but you cannot go, but why? Later that day, Kelly tried to called to her friend Melody and but no one answer, and Kelly thought that probably when out but Kelly didn't know that LA still is quarantine in that city and no one is not permitted to go into that state until it is lift it. So Kelly stick around in New York city and looked up her friend, Colleen, but she was not home, so Kelly sat at the door of her apartment, and wait until she got home but she didn't comes, and wandering if she was infection with the virus. But then decided to go to time square and walks around and there would a lot of peoples on the street but Kelly was getting paranoid, and scare and then stood and watch and a police officer came to Kelly and said are you lost, no I am fine? So what are you are on the street do you know there is a curfew? No, no one didn't tell me about that so you better go inside and you will be safe, so I thought the virus was contain and it was safe, well they didn't tell the whole story, so what is the whole story, there are zombies around, and had not been caught yet! Oh, thanks I will go inside and I will wait for someone to stay with and can you tell me where they took my friend? I think that they took him to the resident lab in Long island, probably was infection, so do you know the address? No I don't, but please go inside, fine I will. Kelly when inside and didn't know but when inside and looked around but it was like stranded and when upstairs, and looked around and then the sirens when off.

So what going on and I need to leave this place but somehow the door was locked and that is great! Now I am stuck in a building that I don't know anyone that lives there! Now what I need to find way out and go to my friend place Colleen, but how I am stuck here! Kelly looked around and so many police cars and military surround the building, now I need to call out, and Kelly called out and they started to shoot at me. Am I so stupid too going into an endemic? Why did I do this and I should tell that I just when into a wrong place and I don't even live here, hope that they will listen to me and I hope I get out of this terrible nightmare and I just want to go home, and then she saw a lady coming toward her she had drool coming out of her mouth and walking weird, well, well, I think that I am big trouble now...what will I do I am trap and I need to called someone on my cell and hope that they will listens to me.

I don't belong I step inside accidental and I should not be in here do you hears what I am saying sir? But you have enter that place and we need to follow the rules and regulation, Kelly but we will try to get you out soon has I speak to commander and what he says, I will take his order and so I am so, so sorry and you are trap with the infection persons in the building, and make sure that you don't touch you or even tried to bite you! You will defense me, I don't have no weapon and I have no ways out and I feel that I am doomed in this situation, be patience and I will tied to help you, please do. I am begging you but I am not able to opens these door to you, so it is very difficult decision that I need to keep you inside right now.

But hurried and I don't know how long it will takes, I am scare and frighten and please get me out, now!!! The sirens when off and then the power was off and then she heard sounds from outside and some were inside and felt like someone was in back of me and I didn't know if I should have stand or move, but then I move very slowly and then Kelly started to walks upstairs and then check the upstairs room and then she when inside and saw Marco, Kelly was about to walks up to him and he looked at her and said, don't come close too me, I am very sick and I do have the virus and you need to leaves this building, but I cannot I am trapped and I should have stay at Colleen Place and I wouldn't be in this terrible situation and I would be safe and now I am here and it is all my fault and I should have not enter here and I should have gone and left this city and never looked back and I was too stupid and then and now alls this time defeat and now I lost, because the police officer told me to go inside a building and I choose the wrong place, I feel really, really stupid but I know that I will find a way out of this place. Go leave this floor, there is the undead roaming the halls, and I don't know if I will find a place to hide until morning, but don't be seen, Kelly those zombies are very hungry and they will eat your brain. I will I am going down and watched your steps and then Kelly saw the spotlight shining and then walks back to the window and said "get me out" now! So far I am not infection and I will be fine and I do have the antidote and I will not be infection, do you understand I did work at the "crystal lab" in LA. That is good to hear Madam, but we have ours order to keep you inside. Well you are making a fatal mistake just let me out. I cannot do this miss, so silent I will shoot you if you tried to escape, what I don't understand, your keeping me inside with the sick.

My dad is in defense and he work for the president, let me out! Enter Quarantine, right now! Step back miss from the doors.

Thin Ice Zombies in LA
Nowhere to Runs or Hide
Quaratine

Day 1

Have you spoke to anyone to get me out of here? I am working on it and I am sorry, yes, and how long will it take and I need to be freed. Do I have to tell you my name and my dad and he really will be pissed and angry that I am trapped here, he will pull rank. Well missy don't threaten me miss, I won't if you let me out and your goon won't shoot me. Miss, well my name is Kelly Anderson and I worked at the Crystal lab and I can help the sick, well even though you might be infection now. Stand back, sure I will, and head will roll, after my dad gets you alls for keeping me in here. Well just listen to what I am saying and you will be fine, sure a bullet in my head and they will says I was infection, no ways I am going to gets out of here if it time alls the time of days do you understand? About one hour later Kelly find a space that she could hide and not get bitten from the infection zombies in the building and Kelly put a stick next the door and make sure that know one would get inside that closet. But what to I do if I am thirsty and I wants to drink and I will be unable to do that's and I will die from thirsts, but also I need to be quiet and not be heard from them and I will all right all night and then Kelly heard a sound that someone came into the building and then they told the peoples to line up and one military man said come out Kelly, so I came out of the closet and I can to the room and then they had equipment and told Kelly to stand on the side and one of them said, we have a opportunity to take you out but first you need to take this shot and Kelly said sure, but what is it? Anti virus syrup, and you will be able to step out, well give too me and but they were wearing face mask and suite and she said why, because of the virus. Ok I am ready and this is better not be a trick and about a minute later, they spotted a

115

zombies and he said we have too hurried because they are coming out and they wants to eat some brains, no I cannot believe that? But come on Kelly don't be such a bitch and let us do our job and you will steps out with us, and Kelly came and took the shot into the arm and Kelly fell to the floor and they carried her out and one of the soldier got jump by the infection one and he wanted to comes out and they shot him to death, and the close the doors and gates to the building and took Kelly to the truck and drove her to the base where her father was and then two hours later, woke up and said how did I get here? No question, my sweet daughter, I do need answers now, but later dear, ok I will not argue with now, I am slight tired and I sleep, and you will be fine in the morning. Kelly fell asleep and said so how is the mission, it going has plans and I think that we have jailed about ten thousand of zombies, at the barrack. But don't says anything to Kelly because she were like to rescue her friends and her friends are zombies and she were get infection, and I take my order and you watch my daughter and you will get the promotion, I am just doing my job sir, and later that day, Kelly woke up and it was very quiet and not a sound, at first Kelly thought that they left her, but no one was there! Kelly got up and looked around but she saw Craig and she asked how where are they? But I cannot answer that is classifying information.

You know I am the captain daughter and you can tell me the information, I cannot tell you miss sorry, I need be secretly and if I told you I would be court martial and put into prisoner, I need to know what going on in case that my dad need me, do you understand and I know how to shoot those zombies. But tell I the detail of the mission and I know how to shoot the weapon and I did fight the zombies over six years and I do have the experience and your dad said not too let you go! Fine I am going alone. Later that night Kelly thought of a plan to sneak out of the base and steal a jeep and meet up with her dad, and fights those zombies, and burns those bodies and get rid of infection. That is a good plan but I know that my will be furious with me but I probably will save his lives and many soldiers. But I am wandering where they went, so let me think and I think they when to the apartment where I been trapped about a day. I will need weapons and grenades and a lot of bullets to shoot those zombies in the head. So soldier where do I get the weapons, shown me where? I told you I cannot do this for you, your dad will shoot me in the head if I let you go to him, at the building. So Kelly got into the jeep and a lot of weapons and bullets and grenades, and stuffs them into the jeep ands said solider boy are you coming with me? He nodded his head and said I am staying at the base. Meanwhile Kelly started up the jeep with the weapons and then the soldier decided to comes and he said wait for me, you are coming hurried. Then they both drove to the city too that building and when they arrival and her dad said what is she doing here? I gave you specify order and you still broke them so I will have to report you too the general for a court martial and I couldn't control your daughter and she is very pushy and now I will get punish for that's! Thanks! For nothing just ruining my life in the military, I will not forget you so you are going too get even with me? No I am just taking order and you refuse and that how she came here sir, that fine! Kelly is a good shooter and we do need her, here. Thanks you have confidence in me and you know that I will do a job and we will prevent them to break out and gun powder to invent them to comes out here and spread the spread too us, and we do make a team, sure we do, dad. But what is the next task that we need to takes to invent the zombies not too comes out of the building, it is shoot to kills. Yes sir, I will follow your order and we will continue watched and sees what they will do, but no change so far, that is good but keeps your eyes on the doors and windows, I sees a breakage in the window that is one I make, are you sure, no but I think so. This is serious business and we need to be in control and focus, yes sir and then Kelly said I need to take a walks around the side of the building and check it out, so make sure there are no leak and no escape, yes I know how that works! Now I am on my ways and make sure that you don't shoot me and tell your sniper not to shoot me, I know Kelly. So Kelly walks very slowly around the building and gave a hand signal that she is there and not to shoot, until I says so. Kelly looked around and then she called them with the cell and told them so far seem like everything looks good and no holes and no leak and I am coming back, and about a minute later, Kelly looks and listens and heard some cans were making noise and she looks and then she saw a six year old boy, but seems normal and Kelly radio and said I am bringing out the boy, and her dad asked is he infection, so far don't have the symptom, so far but be careful and I will dad, my life depend on it. I know that's. About ten minutes later, Kelly and the little boy came out and they took the boy to the hospital for testing and will this child be harm? I don't know if he is infection but we will take care of the problem, well he is a little child and I will go there, no we need you here to guard this building and that is an order do you understand? Yes sir I do, did you reach mom so far she was move to an different location and no even state of California, that good too hears dad and about Molly? I think she is with your mom, the last time I spoke too your mom they were together, and I am glad that you survive the first infection, so am I. but check a watched and be silent now it going to be an blackout and the sirens will go off in ten second from now, good. Then Kelly decided to look around and check if the streets were barb wire and no in and no out, that was the protocol.

So far seems like everything is locked and seem like zombies behind the fence are also locked and scal and there is no ways that they will break out, and Kelly when back and more forces came and now you can sees building burning and fire from rooftop and suddenly they saw a lady on top of the roof and she was yelling and saying help me! They are here, help, help, me! Kelly said I need to get her and her dad said no she could be infection and you stay here, I will send one of my men to rescue her. So can I go along with them, no you stay here do you understand? Yes dad, I will stay here and I won't go, well. Be caution I do all times, Ted and that why I didn't die and I won't dies. Not today and or tomorrow, I will survive this virus and I will fight with my last breathe. Fine and just gets looked and sees if the zombies are secure in the compound and make sure that the electric gate is on also. Yes I will take the pellet gun and tracer if they get out of line, yes but don't get too close, I know the routine and I am not stupid. I didn't says that's! Did I no but be quiet to think what to do if they came out of the compound but I were not be able to shoot them alls. I know and they were comes toward us but we still would not be able to hold them back and so we would lose the battle. So I am coming and I will send a signal and I will called for help and hope that you will comes immediately, sure we will, but why are you lying too Kelly? I am not lying really, put some am, and I don't want to scare her, why not telling the truth, probably were not go on her own, but you can be wrong. Kelly walks very slowly and looked around and no one was around.

Day 2

Kelly approach and looked around and then walks closer to the fence and then she saw Marco and Kelly said "what are you doing here"? I will gets you out, and you will be with me, they will not released me because I am infection and you will catch the virus, and the worst scenario you will become a zombies, so get out of here and leave me alone, I didn't know even that you were here! Your old man didn't tell you what happen? No they caught me in the building where you hid and you thought you were infection but they let you go, I remember that day and I thought you medical help but you just got pack with the zombies. I will get you help no you will not it is too late for me and soon I will be one of them, in one hour and then I will wants to eat your brain, no you will not and I will make sure that you don't, but you cannot open the fence and you will release the zombies, I know what your saying, but I need to help you, no!

Listen too me, I feel the virus moving in my body like a bug and spread through you body and then it make you vomit and then you passed out and then dies. I got the antidote, and I can give a shot and you will be cure. I said no and get out of here and then go back to Ted and he will agree that you took a danger challenger and if you don't I believe that the fence will break and they will roamed the streets and eat yours brains and I will be one of them, I don't want to hears that and I will go.

Kelly started to walks back and Ted called and said get away from you are they are coming!!! Who comes!!! The Zombies are coming they are very near you someone release them and they are going to take us and please runs now and don't looked back, do you have the grenades and shot gun? Yes I do, and then it got silent and Kelly said dad I don't hears you are you ok? Kelly was walking back and then Kelly saw no one was there and Kelly being caution and didn't know what to do at this point. Later Kelly got there and looked around and only saw blood and stains on the ground, and then Ted called out and said hide Kelly now, they can sees you, and smell you. About half hour Kelly heard helicopter and tanks and bomb dropping from the sky and then fires in building and zombies roaming the streets, and saying brains, we wants brains!!!

Brains, we are starving and we wants brains, brains, and I smell you and you have brains and I wants to eat you up and have your brain, you cannot have my brain, and she ran for her life and somehow Kelly got into a truck and being quiet...I will wait until the sun comes up and I need to find Ted and the Greg and I need to find them and I will help them and I hope that they are ok? That night Kelly stay inside that truck and locked it but it was not a good place to hide. I need to find a place that the zombies will not get me and I need to shoot the gun and killed them.

Kelly thought what was being her next move and at that time didn't have a clue what to do. But later that night when I thought it was clear I got out of the truck and walks around and the zombies were not there! At that moment I look for Ted and Greg and I know I needed to find them, right way and I really wanted too sees them I felt alone and I didn't want to be alone, so I search for them and I knew that I wanted to hears his voice. I walks around and looked and then I heard a someone breathing behind me and I looked and it was Ted, but he was not the same.

What wrong, dad? I am infection and I will die and I will become a zombies. No you won't, I will help you, looked behind you, be careful it is Greg and he is zombie? Yes he is? Greg at moment wanted too grab her hand and Ted pull her ways and then he fell to the ground and few minutes and then woke up and got up and wanted to bite her and she push him down and hit him in the head and then ran into the truck and driven away from the place and headed to the highway and then Kelly took the turn and I was surrounded by zombies...now what? I need to think of a plan to get way from this zone, and I don't want too be trapped, and then Kelly realize that the barbwire was on the street and Kelly knew that she had to remove if she wanted to leaves the city.

I cannot believe that I am seal up and I am trapped like a rat and no one to save me but myself...well once again I am alone. I don't like this but I have no choice, but just break the barrack and drove away.

Kelly thought she was in the clear but she was more into the zombie's zone that she probably might not make it alive this time. But hell I am going to fight it and I am going too win this battle and Kelly was thinking how the whole thing started and I am the only can stop it and I need to go back to LA and I need to go to the lab and get it airborne, and but also risking and make the scenario, am I thinking straight and I still planning to go back and maybe will make it worst, well I will not be hurting anyone, everyone else is a zombies. That is true so now I am talking to myself and praying too god that I will be fine. That I will be saving lives and not killing them and I should have stop the testing but I just got to greedy and wanted to have a name in the Newspaper and now the world is suffering. It is my fault and I will never forget myself, and then the phone rang, and I looked and it was Tony and said I need your help and I am locked up in the building and get me out now!!! I just left the town and I am not turning back. Your not going to save your ex boyfriend Tony? Ok, I am coming back and don't make me sorry that I did? Fine!

Kelly turned around and came back to get Tony and then Kelly tried to open the locked door and then the alarm and sirens when off and then Kelly looked and there were soldiers pointed gun at me.

What are you doing? You are not allowed to open those premises, what my friend is inside and I need to help him, and watched they are coming!!! Duck down and they took a fired and shot about twenty zombies at once. Kelly stood and put up your hands and you are under arrest of the government and don't you know who I am?

Day 3

No we don't and you are strict area and we need to remove you immediately and Kelly said, you need me and I need to killed those zombies that killed Ted Ander and he was my father and he worked for the president and now he is dead because the zombies got loose and he became one himself, thank you telling us but you have too leave and we need to destroy the building, you are killing the innocent peoples. No we are not but they are the undead that comes back to lives. End of story Kelly and I am trying to invent that's not your job anymore...

But I defeated the zombies so many times and I didn't dies and I know how to deal with them and how to control them and the rules is too shoot them in the head and if you don't shoot them in the head, they get up and bite your hand off, do you hears what I am saying too? But you are not in control but I am and you are staying and you will not be allowed to leave, I don't need your permission, I will leave! About five minutes later, Kelly walks away and then looked and there would zombies toward coming to Kelly. I need to run and but they started to shoot at me and I duck and they almost got me and I were been eaten up by the zombie and probably turn into one, then Kelly when back to the general and said what are you doing shoot at me? I was not at you but at the zombies. Fine you scare the shit out of me and I don't wants this too happen again do you hears what I am saying too you, sir? Yes loud and clear, good and now I will be leaving this quarantine area and go back to my Lab and work on more antidote, do you gets it, yes I do but you are not allow to leave, I am going if you are going to shoot me? Then she went the red van and got inside and drove away and the military started to shoot at her and she said don't shoot at me, I am pissed enough, just let me do my work. Kelly drove away and then the storm brew and Kelly had to drive into tornado and the wind that almost flew away and then Kelly stops and thought I need shelter and then no I am staying in the van and then she saw them approaching her... said I need gets out location and contact the team, and get rid of zombies, and stop the virus. For once and alls!

Then Rick approach her and you cannot do it yourself I will come along and help you, I don't need your help, I survive this virus on my own. But I wants too come along, I don't need you, fine but I am still coming!!!

They both got inside the van and drove away, but they both argument, then they drove off the road. What are doing? You are distracting me and I need to focus and we need to get there in three days. Kelly drove so fast and how your driving you will kill us. I won't kill us I am trying too save us. Not how you driving and not paying too the road, yes I am. Don't yell at me! All the way to LA, Kelly didn't speak too Rick and they made a few stop signs on the ways. On the first stop seems to be normal. They looked around no zombies around, any sight of zombies but they would safe, they thought! Then Rick saw something was around the corner, saw two zombies, coming toward them. Do you see them, not exactly Rick. About five minutes, more would coming closer get into the van, now. Kelly like jump inside and Rick step inside and Kelly started up the van and drove away that was very close called, I know. Then they decided to stop to get gas and Rick said is that a good idea, no? Ok I will take your advice and we have about two thousand and half too LA, so will make it. Not sure we are going on with lot obstacles in the ways. But we cannot do anything about it but we will make it with no problem, yes, but we will figure it out and it will not be easy but don't worry your head about it, you are worry wart, now you are calling me names, that I will kick you out of my van and you will walks. Don't threaten me, I am not; leave me alone, I will. I don't want to speak with you, just leave me alone, fine. Then the second stop, Kelly stop the van and I need to stretch my feet and I will looks around and I will be back in five, but don't leave me behind, I won't leave you, I promise. Rick walk behind the building looked around and Rick didn't looked around but he didn't sees them coming, they would coming closer and closer and Kelly decided to go to Rick and saw them near him, Kelly, said watched out they are going to bite you and no they won't get me and he started to runs and then they spotted her and they saw her and she started to runs to the van and but looked for Rick and Kelly didn't sees him, and Kelly called out his name and but he didn't answers her and then a rear of her eye and he was standing in back of her. So what wrong with you, i am fine and what do are you saying that I got bitten by the bug? Maybe you did, no I have not so let me give you a test and sees if you are not infection, do it. Kelly took out the kit and drew some blood and then put the stick into the capsule and then shakes it and then if it turns green that you are not sick, so are this test 100 percent or are they give the wrong reading? So far you don't looks sick but we cannot stand here because they are coming and I don't have gunpowder so we need to get away now, fine I am ready and I don't wants to be "dead Meat' I don't neither, let go!! They both got inside and Kelly said I forgot something behind and I will be back in five, but hurried I will, and meanwhile back, at the building the zombies were breaking through the doors and the soldiers, were shooting at them but some were just getting too close to comfort, and we don't have powers too stops them. But sir we will get killed but I cannot do anything about that's!

Then back to Kelly and Kelly walks toward the place behind the building and felt like someone was watching her, and then Meanwhile Rick was looking out for Kelly too come back and it seem too long and left the van. At that moment, Kelly turned around and they were standing right next to her and said now what? Then Rick approach and said, this time I will save you, I don't need any saving from anyone and not from you, well you are being such a bitch! No I am not... come here counted of ten and I will watch your back, thanks! But be very slowly and don't looked at them, I am not and make sure that they cannot reach you, looks one is behind you and don't let him get you, I won't said Rick. I will watch your steps. About a minute, I got what I drop and you come too me now. Ok I am coming and more are coming and we need to runs from here, now. They started to runs to the van but Rick slip and landed in front of one of the zombie and Kelly looked back and now what? Be quiet and try not to let him sees you drag under him and slowly get up and runs for your life. Got up and then the zombie grab him and then Kelly came and pull him off him and then the zombie grab Kelly and once again Rick pull it off her and got a slight bite, and then they both ran to the van and drove off and Rick tried to hide the bite from Kelly and Kelly asked what wrong? Nothing! Are you sure? Yes don't lies too me. I am not showing me your hands, why? I need to sees if you didn't get bitten and I can help you not get the virus. Ok I shown you and you will give me the antidote, not sure at this point and but if I sees sign of the virus, then I will give you the antidote, fine, and meanwhile it will be in my blood stream, yes, otherwise I give you the shot now, it won't works! Be patience and I will use for the last resort and you will not be a zombies. So let talked about what we will do when we get to the lab and hope no one is guarding the lab, hope not! But we have couples more days to get there and then we have one or two stop for foods and fuel for the van and then we will be on ours ways. Kelly started to looked at Rick and he was fast asleep but his face was like pale and then he opened his eyes and they were like bloodspot and ugly and Kelly didn't wants to says anything too him but she was silent and then he started too act not normal but then he tried too bite me and I hit him and stops the van and threw him out and then he was saying what are you doing? You are infection ands it is too late to help you so you have lied too me from the start no, I was out of antidote and that why I didn't give too you. Lady every word you says was a lies and I don't you understand that I am dying and I am going to be a zombies, but I still can help but I need to tied you up until I get to the lab and give you a shot.

But it will be too late and I need it now, know but I have a stronger dosage in the lab that if someone in effect for five hour bite, but it will be much longer and it might not works. But do you still want to come along but I will put in the back in case you die, ok! Will it be too long no I don't know I don't have answer for that question right now? So Kelly tied him up and watched him alls the ways to LA. Then she heard sound his sound and he was trying to get loose. Stops it now, I will shoot you!! I will.

Day 4

We are almost there but not exactly, so what does that mean? So Rick I took the wrong exit and now we are going toward San Diego and not LA and we will not get there on schedule and you probably will be a zombies. So looked Kelly there are zombies on the highway and I don't know if I can pass them but I will try. At that moment the zombies were getting closer and closer to us. Then Rick said I will become one and I will just drop me off and then I will let them chase me and you will be able to take the right route and get away, but the whole point is too get you there and cure you. Seems like it not going too happened at this point and you give up on me, and I am not going to let you do that do you understand. Rick? Yes I do and I don't wants you too go out there, and I will not let you loose and so we are going to fight them off ourselves. Don't you think that you might be making a fatal mistake and even died and I am willing take a chance and saving million lives. That is true and I will save if those don't get us first and we need to passed them and not let them get us that is the plan but I think not such a good plan. Do you have a better plan, Rick? I don't and I don't wants to argue with you anyone and I just wants to get heal and killed off that bastard that wants our brains. But seems like they are getting stronger and they are remember what they did in the past and now they are doing that's! Know but I don't want to be around them and they smell us and they wants to eat our brains. Don't let them hears you breathe, and tried to be quiet, Rick. Meanwhile at the building the soldiers were trying off to killed off the zombies but they were started to beat the soldiers in numbers that was a losing battle and the general somehow he snuck away and when into jeep and started up and left his men too fight with the zombies and he tried to go on a different streets but there were barbwire and he couldn't go through so he got out of the truck and pull it out and a thousand of zombies came toward him. The general ran for his life but the zombies caught up too him and started to tear him into pieces, and ate his brain. One of the soldier heard him too called for helped but when the soldier approach him, he saw the zombies coming toward him and he ran so fast that he was out of breathe and told the other soldiers it was time to leaves immediately this area. Kelly and Rick were not too far from the lab and Kelly said you save me so many times but now I see that you are turning into a zombie, and I have no choice but too killed you. Rick begged her not too shoot him, and Kelly said I have too. You said you were save me! I did but we will be too late to give you the syrup that you need and it is called k 110. But you need to let me try it before I am a zombie. Yes I did promise you and I do keep my promises, too my friends. About two hour later they were near the lab and there were bunch of soldiers watching the building and we need to get inside and take the antidote. Yes! I do agree with you but how do we do it? Well we need to make a distract and I get inside and you will wait for me out here, maybe we can both go inside and don't let them sees us and I start a fire and they will go too it. That is a plan and I like it very much, Rick, and it probably will work, I hope so. "The plan is that we use a service elevator in the back and we need to go on floor 2130 and get the antidote and take a lot and then help out the infection stage one, but if you are beyond stage one it will not work. Why are you telling me? Well it is too late for you, Rick and I did warns you not too get bitten, yes you did but you also told me that you were help me, I just needed you too get me here and you did and now I need to get something from my pocket and then she pull out the gun and shot him with the silencer in the head and he fell to the ground ands said why did you killed me? Then he closes his eyes and died. Kelly has tears in her eyes and said sorry my dear friend, but you were going to be a zombie, and I had no choice, and gave him a kiss on the lips.

"Then Kelly walks way and then when into the room a and check the files said antidote and took couple bottle and when into the hall and then step into the elevator and she was about too push the elevator, and Kelly saw zombies coming toward her and Kelly said I need to push the button and go down and I am not going to be stuck here with zombies not this time around, no ways! But the doors were stuck and Kelly was really getting nervous that the door were not close and now what and then they close and Kelly was relief, and she got downstairs and she was stops by the military and said you under arrest and for trespass and then said don't you know who I am? No madam, you are on government property and then she shown them her name tag and said sorry missy. You are coming with us and you will explains to the president and what happened to your dad and it is a long story so we were like too hear it. Fine the zombies killed him. At the place in New York City were that building was quarantine and I was trap there for few hours and I got release and send to get the antidote and save some peoples. Do you know that you could be infection with that virus? Yes I been told but I am fine. We cannot let you go until we test you and remove the item in your hand and come over here, yes sir. So Kelly said where are you taking me, well we are taking you too the base and testing you, but you are wasting time on me and I need to go there and rescue the sick and helpless and give them a fighting chance, so take her and they put handcuff on her hands and you are going too pay, colonel, no I am not I am invent the spread. Time is running out for you sir, and I am the only hope that you got! Take her away and put her into the truck and drove away on route 80 away from the lab and Kelly tried to get away and the soldier was pointed the gun at her. But somehow Kelly remember that she had a key in her pocket and unlock and kept quiet and then snuck up the soldier and hit him on the head and jump out of the truck and snuck in front of the truck and got the antidote and ran quick to her van and drove away and then the colonel came ands said where is Kelly? I don't know sir she hit me and she was gone! Fine you will get court martial for letting a prisoner too escape. Take him from me and he will be charge with treason and helping that Kelly person too escape, maybe I should just shoot him now, what wrong with you colonel? One of the soldier said he must be infect and he must becoming a zombie, we should shoot him. No I am not going too do that unless that he change, I agree with you. Later that night Kelly was driving on the 80 near Los Angeles, and Kelly was getting a bit tired and stop at the motel and took out the antidote and gave her and shot and rest in the car and almost fell asleep, and then Kelly put on the radio to make sure that she was not fall asleep. On the "special report" they said that the undead are still coming back too lives. Now there are more than thought and it is really dangerous to be out in the night". Now Kelly got out of the van and when inside of the lobby and it was stranded. And she rang the bell and no one came, and Kelly looked around and saw body parts everywhere that she looked. Kelly said too herself that she must go now and get out of that quick and no stopping nowhere, at alls. Now Kelly was alone and no one around to protection her and alls her friends were dead and didn't know where too go and be safe. How Kelly was frighten and scare and hungry and cried, with a lot of tears falling from her eyes and I then thought to herself and that I am not going to dies, not today or tomorrow. When Kelly was driving, she saw zombies and peoples screaming for there lives but Kelly didn't have a weapon or strength to fight, but also Kelly didn't want to give up on life. But Kelly kept on going and now Kelly was getting pale and her long red hair and her green eyes were she was about five feet and seven inches tall and she was medium build and some what attractive. At this point Kelly was alone and sad and didn't have a friend that time of her life. One point of her life that she felt that she was about drive into the ocean, but then she thought, I am not a quitter. So Kelly park her van near the beach and close the doors and then fell asleep and about five hour later, someone knock at the door and at that moment, Kelly scream and scare at the same moment. At first she didn't wants to talk with him but him convenience her then she slowly open the door and he started to speak and he said his name was Al and he is from North Hollywood, and he asked her what was her name? My name is Kelly and what do you wants from me? Nothing maybe a glass of waters some foods; don't know that there are zombies out there? Yes I do and I am the zombies control patrol and said you must be kidding me? No I am not. Comes out Kelly and let me take you too the safe zone and you will meet my friends and they are not sick and we fight off the zombies, I don't know and I don't trust you, that is true. Comes before it gets dark and they will be out there! I know they will be. So Kelly decided to trust Al and follow him too his hideout and Kelly was not sure.

Day 5 Last day of the quarantine

But Kelly just looked around and was very preserve about her surround, when she approach the condo, and walk very slowly and there were ten person and they seems like they were not infection and normal that what Kelly thought and that she would be fine with Al and his friends, but Kelly didn't know what were happened next? Kelly looked around and said well this is a nice place and so how long has stayed here? Not too long but would anyone had symptoms of a virus? No one in our group and we didn't go out months. What do you means? I don't understand what you are saying. Al said that we are the peoples that are affecting by the sun and so we just stay inside, I still don't understand. So if you do stay you need to follow ours rules and what is that's! Well not opening the window shades and door during the day! I can do that but can I catch it from you, no you cannot and don't be afraid of us, I am not! Later that night Kelly said well I am bit exhaust and I need to rest and Al said I will show you, your room. My room that what I said and when we go out you must closed the door behind us, and we when knock we will give you a signal of three knocks. But we need to warns you of a old lady next door, she is wicked and she will wants too eat you up, I don't understand do open the door for her, I won't! Al and his friend's walks out of the door and Kelly locked and when into her bedroom and slept for hours and she woke up and they still were not there! Kelly looked around and still no one in sight and then she looked outside and then she saw them being chase by the zombies, and Kelly thought how can I helped them, when I am trap inside? About two hours later, Al came back and knocks at the door and Kelly listens if he gave the signal first, and then she let him in. When he came inside he was spread with bloods on his clothes and been bitten by the zombies and then rest are roaming the streets of LA. Kelly asked what happened to your friends, they got caught and bitten by the zombies and then Kelly said I thought the quarantine was lifted. I guess the government is not telling us the truth about what going on in the world. So what condition are you? What do you means? Did the zombie bite you? Not sure I didn't feel a thing. So let me check you out but first close the curtain. Then Kelly looked at his hands and they were fine and then she looked at his arms two were bitten but not only today but before, and Kelly said you have been bitten before but seem like you are not affect with the virus. Someway I am and someway I am not, I don't understand? But you are a zombies but you got some kind of antidote and they prevent to progress has the rest of your friends and they will be coming back but I think you make me has there meal that they were not feed off you, is that right that why you bought me here? Yes they will be coming soon and I will hide in my room and you don't leave. I am trapped and I did trust you but in some way you betray me. How could you I could have helped you and your friends and now you put me into jeopardy and I have no place too hide but here. But they will eat me up and turned me into a zombie, even worst I will be torn limb to limb and I will be in couple part and I will drag myself to feed on brains. I sees your eyes are very affect and I sees the colors in your eyes and you need to let me leave this place, I cannot they will killed if I do. I am there servant. Then Kelly when inside her room and thought she was able to lock the door but she couldn't, so she decided to use a chair against the door and Kelly knew that she couldn't keeps them out for long so she decided to open the window and it were not open and Kelly tried for hours. But Kelly didn't give up and then she tried to open the other window and it pried open and took some sheet and climb out the window and make sure that she were reach the bottom floor. When Kelly reaches the ground floor she stuck there the bushes and headed to the Hollywood bowl. Meanwhile Al thought that Kelly was still in her room taking a nap, about half hour later his friends came back and they were bloody and horrible on there faces. Then they asked Al where is Kelly and he said she is sleeping and one of his friends said we need to wake her up and have her brains, now! Al said I will get her and I will bring her too you my friends. So Al tried to unlock the door but it was stuck and he pushes inside and she was not there, and then notice the window was open, and then Al called out and she is not here, I thought you were watching her, I was. So where is she? I don't know, so don't you remember what we said if she was gone, you were be dead meat, but how can you eat your friend? I thought you wouldn't eat me but I can find others out there, but we are hungry for your brain, and you are the one that we want now. Wait a minute, I will be right back and you that I will be, so how do we know if you will comes back? You don't but you better let me go! Don't threaten me, do you understand? Yes I do and then Al somehow mange to sneak away and close the door behind and ran out of the building and didn't looked back and kept on running and then Al stops and in the alley then he saw the zombies and he ran the opposition direction toward the highway and then he saw Kelly. Then he called out too Kelly and said why did you runway and she said I am not going to be dead meat and be eaten up by zombies.

No ways and I am going too the "Hollywood bowl and I am going to go back to the lab and get the cure and be safe. I am going back there and I am going too and I think I will be able to helped you, I don't wants your helped because I cannot trust you, you wanted to feed me too your zombies, friend. I will not do this again and I am not going back but if I turned you need to shoot me in the head and I know the drill, and it happened over and over my friends died and I was alone and I defeated the odd in the zombies battle, about you? Well my odd were not so good has yours but I am still here but I am partly zombies, and the living. But I want to be cure and go back to my family if they are alive. Yes, I agree!

Day 6 Zombies everywhere in sight!

Kelly said the quarantine was lifted and the streets with thousand and thousand of zombies and no one around to killed them, and I think that we are alone with the population of the zombies. About the living instinct and that is really bad for us and seems like they are taking over the world.

But we need to change that and we need not too get sick and no we need too find the no one are not infection and gets rid of the zombies. You right but where are the military men, and I don't hears any shooting and then no bomb going off and where are the missiles, we sure need some now, and I have no clue how we will get through those zombies.

Well maybe we can go can somehow go around them and but they still would smell us…that is true. So what are we going to do exactly? I don't know but they are very near, and I feel the walking toward us and I think that sees us and I think that we should runs but they are everywhere, I know. Do we go straight or turn left or right I don't know how to answer your questions but I know that we cannot stand in the middle of the street and we need to run now… so are you coming? Yes I am they are approaching us very close and do you think that we will reach the van and drive away and go toward the highway, can we go through them of course we can? Kelly runs to the van and I will wait until you started up the van and then we will leave LA. Kelly got to the van and started it up and drove up to AL and said get inside and Al said no I am staying and Kelly said you are wasting time and we need to go now. But Kelly refuse too leave Al and Kelly stops the van and pull him in and said why? I belong here, why get me I wanted you too were safe, I know you do but I also don't wants to be alone with the zombies. Later that day Kelly and Al drove through the zombies and somehow one zombie got on the van and didn't shake him off the van and he was still on the roof. Now what well I make a sharp turned and then he will fell off the van and we will be all right! So far the zombie tired to get into the van and somehow she curve and turned the wheel but the zombie was in the back of the van. Zombie was about too grabbing Kelly somehow Al pull the zombie arm and threw him in the back of the van. The doors open wide and everything flew out and that great! Our supplies are lost and we will have no foods and water is gone, but we will find more supplies. Will it be safe the foods and the water that I had it were tested and it was good? Now we might get the virus because that zombie that got inside the van and it really screw up ours supplies and now we can be screwed being careless and I know but I believe that we will be fine and nothing too worry about, but you mention the helicopter pad and where is it location and maybe we can fly out of here. I don't remember where that place is but I think it is near the farmer market and near the CBS studio, so why don't we go there? So I take route 80 to which freeway and I been there a long time ago and I think that we should find that place and get the hell out of here. Give me a map and I want to get there before the night fall. Ok let find it and what the hurried with you suddenly, so your friends might be after and you are afraid that you will be dead meat for them. Yes, yes and I don't wants to be here any long don't you agree, and I hope it is running, please don't jinx us Al. what did I says! But Kelly drove fast and didn't stops on lights and stop on stop sign and just drove like a mad woman that had too get there in a hurried. Kelly are you alls right seem like you are not breathing? I am fine, but I feel a little scare and paranoid, but I am not since the virus I became frighten. But relax and we will get there in one piece, yes and then we will not too fight with the zombies, yes and we can have normal lives. Have a family and take walks in the park and have picnic with friends and I do missed the good old days!

Will it ever be the same that Kelly asked Al I don't know but I know that we cannot stick around here because this area is more populations then the rest and I did seen them here mores here and I almost got caught here, escape once and the second time got bitten and then I was a little sick but somehow my immune system was not weak and it fight off the virus.

Kelly said that is your story about the zombies but my story that I had work at the lab that was working on the antidote and then some got infection and they became zombies and I escape my work place and I thought it were stop in the lab but the vents were open and peoples got sick and they were dying around and know one couldn't stop this virus and so when the alarm when off and I just put on the protection suit and walks out and walks too the garage and drove away and miles and miles away and then there was a special report that everyone should lock there doors and windows and at that moment I knew it was the virus that spreads rapidly and I didn't have the cure for anyone but few antidote.

Then I got stuck in a building and they were shooting at me and I told them I was the general daughter and they check it out and I was freed and then my dad wanted me to go back home and I fight in a few battle and then my mission and I got back too LA to gets the high protein antidote, but my mission fail and I got here and been surrounded by zombies and then you caught me too be fed by your zombies. I am really sorry about that's but I had no choice, yes you did I was there servant to them, no reason too get me has dead meat for your friends.

Just forget the past and now it is the present and we need to find a plane and helicopter to leave this city. Comes on keeps on driving and don't go so fast and I just wants to be safe and I don't know where that is but I know that we will find it. They drove to the LAX airport and Al said why here? Well they have planes and maybe we will find a copter to escape this nightmare, I do agree totally but will we run into zombies here? I am not sure said Kelly but I think that we can stay here for the night. Ok if you say so, I will agree with you. Fine, so do me!

Day 7 LAX ways out of the city of zombies

We are almost there and I will drop you off the terminal five and you will looked around, so are we taking a flight out, not sure at this moment.

But Kelly said make sure, I will check around the terminal, no sight and no zombies, that are good. Al said I looked around once again, good and that we must be on guard, you are right. So Kelly and AL, now we need to get on the second level, and looking around and sees if it clear and we can stay here for the night, I agree with you and I will be there in minute.

I will be waiting for on top of the stairs, fine! I see you soon. Meanwhile looks around the lobby and checks every corner and spotted a little girl and called out to her, but she ran and when after her, then she surrounded by the zombies. Now what? What will I do I cannot reach Al and I will get bitten, and become worst scenario, and nightmare that I am having right now! Al was thinking why she is being so long, I need to sees what going on and I need to check up on her. So Al started to walk down the stairs and walking toward Kelly and saw those zombies surround Kelly and AL pull out the gun and started to shot at the zombies, and bend down Kelly. So Kelly bend down he almost hit her and at that moment she said are you crazy trying too killed me? No, but it seems like it.

No one had control of them and we would have a difficult task to of getting rid of the zombies, but we didn't have lot bullets to shoot them. But we would going to tried to killed them and be safe and not be eaten up and then we heard a lady voice the corner of the terminal and she called out and she said my name is Vicky and can you helped me? Yes we can so comes over here, I am scared and I think there is one in back of me and I am afraid to move. We will be right, just sit tight and you will be right there! Meanwhile Kelly and Al would coming closer to Vicky and Vicky was hiding but she felt they were getting closer and closer, and think that they were not comes on time, but somehow they passed the zombies and came to rescue Vicky. Vicky was relief and said her friends were someplace in the terminal and don't know where they went? But Kelly and Al said we will find them but we need to stick together and do you understand what I am saying? Yes I don't want to be traps with the zombies anymore and I just want out too gets out of here, now! We will wait for Kelly, yes we are, but I do wants. Too meet up with them, don't go alone they might be infection with the virus and maybe became zombies. I am not standing around and wait for Kelly too comes, I am ready to take the steps to the second level, but we have not check it out and you might get bitten and be dead, I will be very careful and I will watched my step. Meanwhile Kelly, called out too Al and said I will be there in five minutes and I wants to talked with Vicky and then Al said just left the front and when on the second floors I told you not too let her go! But Vicky refuse too listen and so I cannot do anything to help her that is true. But I am going to find a ways out of here and I think that roof might be the right place too is? I am not sure at this point. So AL waited for Kelly too comes and meanwhile Vicky started to go beyond the zone and Vicky notice it was getting pitch black and didn't wants to walks back to the lower terminal and now Vicky once again was alone what might happened, she heard footsteps in the background and thought it was Kelly and Al and then it got louder and louder and they were "saying that they wanted "Brains, brains, brains, and now Vicky duck under the stairs, and thought that they were not sees her. Vicky was about too turned around and then one of the male zombie, grab her hand and bite it off, and then another got her leg and she was bleeding and more zombies came to feed on her. Later that day and Kelly and Al said, we have not heard from Vicky, hope that she is fine? I don't know there are many zombies around here. I think we should look for her now I think that she might be in trouble, but I did warn her. Yes you did and it is not your fault and just forgets about it and we will search for her and hope that we don't have to deal with the zombies. But I think that we will have too and I think that Vicky is a goner and we shouldn't even looked for her, so you are saying that we should just abandon her and leave this place without her? Yes, exactly that what I am saying too you, so you would leave me too, if you couldn't find me? Yes, but I wouldn't and now I know where I stand with you so I better not go too far and you might just leave and I will be alone to fight the zombies. No, I would not do that to you and I think that you were and don't lies too me. I won't! They walks a bit like two miles on the second level of the terminal and they looked around and no sight of Vicky. I told you that Vicky probably got bitten and became a zombie. You don't know that maybe she met up with her friends and they got away from here. Well we really don't know and I am not going to fight with you about thing that might not be true. I don't know what going what happened too us but I hope that we survivor this virus. I also agree with you, Al. But keep a good watched and make sure no surprises like attack from the zombies. Sure I am being focus and also a little infection and I could lost it myself you know and you will need to shoot me in the head. I will have no problem about doing that's! A little ways out, Al saw Vicky and he called out her name, and Kelly said what have you done? I just wanted to let Vicky that we are here. I didn't do anything wrong, did I? Well, don't you see what you have done...? Alls those zombies are coming toward us and you started this because you called out for Vicky. Now they will get us and we will dies and it alls your damn faults because you were looking for that slut. Sorry, but I thought she were be all right!

Now we going to fight with them and I don't know if we are going to win this fight and there are too many of them. About hour later, Kelly was on the roof and Al was still fighting off the zombies and trying to open the hatch door to the roof and it was locked and wouldn't unlock the door.

Help Me Please

Kelly do you hears me? No answers, and from Kelly, and Al knock at the door and no one came too the door and then the zombies were getting very near too AL and this can be happening, too me, Kelly do you hears me? Then the hatch open and said get inside here hurried now... did they bite you are you fine, I think that I am not feeling that great! So you did get bit and now I am will be alone and no one to loves, but I am not going too leave you, do you understand? I will help you and I will wrap the cut and I will make it better. Well, I will check my pocket for the antidote and you will not feel the change but you still might be a zombie anyway, so are willing to take a chance and take the shot and hang around with me, said Kelly. About half hour later, Kelly said I think you are changing and you are infection and they are coming too the rooftop and I will be trap and no escape from here, and you told me that probably a helicopter would be here and it not and I am doomed. So many years I survive and now you got me into this situation that I will dies, thanks! I will get you out of here and I have park the van near the terminal B and it is in front of the door so you need to get out of here and run into the zombies, no thanks! You cannot stay here Kelly and don't boss me around neither, do you understand? So you are wasting time just staying here and I will distract them and you can go to the lower level and they can be everywhere and I will still be trap. Stop, stop that's being so negative, and you are strong and you will be able, and you will get too the van and drive, toward the San Diego, and keeps driving and don't stops and first I need too get off the roof and get to the lower level and I told you that I will help you and then you will be alone. That is true but I will take you, and I will be a zombie, about twenty

139

minutes, and still I have time. Understand when you get inside and the van and you will lock the doors and drive away. Yes I will and I will not look back and I will find a safe house and then I will found other peoples that will help me too survive. Just keep on thinking and you will be fine and then we will tells the military what happen in the lab, probably the military are fighting off the zombies and maybe they are zombies. Don't says that Kelly that is probably the truth, and no lie. I am ready too leave and you make sure that I have a clear way too escape and I won't be caught, sure, I will really tried.

In one minute, I will open the hatch, I will looked out and then I will tells you when it time to step out and you run has fast has you can, promise me, Kelly said sure! Al looked out and then said ok it is time too get outside and you can step out now, and leaves. Will you be fine? Yes don't worry about me, I will be silent and they will not hear me! Sure. I am going and I am going to get help and you will go to the hospital and you will be fine. Just go and don't looked back and go, go, go, fine I am going. Kelly left and didn't looked back and Al got attack by Zombies and he is gone!

**Thin Ice Zombies in LA
Nowhere to runs or hide!
Sole Survivor**

Survivor

Now I left Al about one hour ago and I somehow I survive the attack from the zombies and I knew that Al was gone and now I felt really alone and I drove with a lot tears and crying and no one to talked too and no one, but only myself and now I don't know where I am going end up and I know that I don't have a lot of fuel for my van but I hope that I find someone, that is not a zombie, and the night will comes soon. I will need a place too sleep and I will need to find a place too sleeps and I am really tired and hungry, and about a second I saw more zombies coming toward me. But I am not going to stop and I am just keep on going and I will find a shelter and I will be fine tonight and then I heard planes and helicopters above my head and I think that they were save me but they started too shoot at me and I started to drive faster, and I just took the wrong turn and I almost ended up in a ditch. I did stop for a moment and looked around and I thought it were been ok but suddenly the zombies came and I felt trap but somehow I dash through them and I drove away. That was really close. Then I saw a man standing on the sidewalk and he was daze and confuse and was not sure what was wrong with him, but I did stop and I started too talked with him and I asked him is name and he said Jimmy Gold and I asked why he was standing there and he was looking for his friends, but they never show up. I told him that I would help him too find his friends and Jimmy said I am looking for my friends that when to LAX and they left me behind and said that they were be back in one hour and never came back, so can you give a description of them, well one was like a dirty blonde and about five feet and six inches tall and have blue eyes, and her name is Vicky. Oh I sees, but we cannot go to the airport because, thousand of zombies there! But I must find her, but why, I am not sure, but I think that she was special in my life and I don't wants too lose her, I think that you did all ready! I don't wants to hears that's! But that is the truth and she is a zombie. I don't believe you, you could be lying too me, and keep me away from LAX. No, I don't even know you and I will take you and you can sees for yourself but it is very danger situation that I will do be doing for you but I will. So Jimmy got into the van and Kelly said hold on tight, we will go through a lot of zombies on the ways, sure, I could handle it. Jimmy sat in the car and looked and looked and he couldn't believe his eyes, and Kelly thought to herself that probably too see if that Al was alive and were save him somehow, with Jimmy helped. When they arrive to LAX and Kelly said are you sure that you wants too go inside and runs into zombies? Yes I have no choice, the woman of my life, could be trap and I were like too save her, I do understand and I think it probably a slim chance. I don't wants to hears that, so be quiet, sure I could leave you here, I think that you were not do that to anyone, and I believe that you were stay until we find her, yes I would, but don't worry about it and I will watched out for the zombies if they are coming close. Yes you are the expert and I believe that we will make it out alive and we will alls go to the safe heaven and we will be safe there, well I did that's and really there is no place like that's! Are you ready to step inside the terminal and check out if you can find your friend, so are you coming? I am not sure. I cannot go alone, please come with me, fine, I will! About ten minutes later they were inside and so far we are fine and so we can check each level. But Kelly I am not going alone, you are coming with me and don't ever threaten me, do you understand? Sure I do, and I will walks out and leave you here, now you are threaten me and stop this, said Jimmy, I thought I saw someone walking she was wearing the blue blouse and blue jean like Vicky, I need to follows her, sure go for it. I will be here! Meanwhile Kelly thought, am I stupid too bring Jimmy here and looked for some character Vicky, she could be zombie, and I bought danger too myself and Jimmy. Kelly stood and looked around and Jimmy follows that woman to the third floor and he looked around and then, he saw her and she was not the same has he remember her, drool were coming out of her mouth and blood on her hands and then she started to says, I wants your brain, brain, brain, and he somehow he yelled out on the balcony and Kelly heard him and she took the elevator to the third floor, and pull out the gun and shot the zombie in the head and then Kelly said, let go! Jimmy said I am ready to go and I will be right back of you, good. But they are coming, closer, closer, too me. But hurried I am coming but don't fall back, I am not. Jimmy said it is my fault now we are in danger, and hope that we make alive, we will don't worry, we will not gets caught, I have a gun too shoot the zombies in the head, survive this ordeal. Kelly said soon that we will out of the terminal, watched each corner, I will Jimmy, he reply. Kelly was about too open the door, the zombies standing there, and we need to go the other exit, on the other of terminal, but it will be far from the van.

Don't worry; I will make it, so how to do know it is? We have about ten minutes to gets there, and that sound good, but I think that we are not alone; Kelly said I know the zombies are inside and we are trapped. Come on I am in back of you, good. They reach the other exit and it was clear, but the zombies, would behind them so gets out of door and close the door. I did but seem like the door is opening, they are coming outside, we need to keeps them inside, and do you understand? Kelly and Jimmy, were walking away from the terminal, and walking toward the car. Then three zombies jumped out and Jimmy said they got me, help me, I will, and Kelly rush to help and punch one of them and fell down and Kelly poke the zombie in the head. Then the second one approach Kelly and she shot him in the head and fell to the ground, and two zombies would dead and third approach Kelly. Then Kelly whack the zombie and it fell to the ground and Kelly thought it was the end of them, but she was wrong and Jimmy said I wanted to sees Vicky and now we are in trouble and don't worry about your head about it, about five minutes later, they got to the van and they got inside but somehow one zombie grab jimmy leg, and almost bite it off. Kelly said, are sure that you are not hurt? No I am not, so we are on our ways of this place and no looking back, got it? Later that night they drove for hours and hours and but no place was safe to stay for a night. So what should we do and where to go and then Jimmy said I have a friend and his name is Frank and he lives in the Beverly Hills and maybe we can go there? So how far from the hills so do used route 80 too get too him? Yes we do and I show you the ways. But I am getting a bit tired and so I want to rest for a while, is that a good idea, right now? I think so and I want to runs of the cliff, ok we will be staying here for a while, great! Kelly took a snooze and Jimmy was looking out for zombies and pirates that stole from peoples, and so jimmy was a bit frighten sitting in the car but the car was locked and Jimmy was playing with the radio but nothing was on the station, so he turned it off and then suddenly Kelly woke up ands said what going on here? I thought I saw peoples walking around us but I must been just alls in my mind, hope that you are right?

Jimmy what wrong with you? I am fine, but you looked kind of pale, are sure that you didn't get bitten by the zombie, tell me the truth, I won't shoot you in the head, not yet! Thanks a lot, no I am not infection but I think I am a bit paranoid about the zombies, thing, so am I but we do stay alive, and try to win the battle and not ending up being dead meat.

I am with you and I don't wants to die and I just want to make it too tomorrow and see another day! I feel the same said Jimmy and let go and not looked back and so they kept on driving and Jimmy said that we are running out of gas and we will not find another around. Hope that you are wrong and I don't wants to be stranded out here with a bunch of zombies that wants to eat my brain, I don't neither, so far do get away from this zombies world. But we are the living and the rest are the undead that roamed the earth with us ands seems like they are winning the war, and we are losing it, don't says that Kelly. But you need too hear the truth and that alls that we are defeated and probably will end of dead. But they drove a little more and then the car stall and now what? So we walks and find a place too stay and think what ours next move... ok with me but I don't know how long that we will survive the zombies, and I am going too let them win no ways! I know that you are strong Kelly but I might drag you down and I don't wants to do that's! Jimmy said you should have left me on that corner and let me dies, no I will not listens too what you are saying! You need to listens to me and you will live and then we will find that safe place where no zombie's lives, and then we can have a normal life, but we are stranger and we are not lover, said Kelly. After this we will go our separate life and so you will probably looking for your family somewhere out there! Yes I will!

No End to the Zombies

We still have a situation that might not end tonight but I am willing to risk and stay at the building that was quarantine building and stay there and probably no one were except us too stay there. But we could be seeing zombies and being surrounded by them, so do you wants to take a chance and stay here, for the night and then we will travels in the morning and this ways we will sees them coming!!! We need to watched two sides and then steps out and then looked around and then walks too the van and then drive away, and then we will go to a city that is not affection and then we can stay there. But for now we need to stay here and then gets some bullets and guns that we can fight and killed them off. Will we ever get rid of them and sometime I feel that we won't and that is not good, and I think that we need to find a plan. Did think of plan for escape, no not exactly but soon, and I don't want to lose anymore lose anymore friends, I don't neither, but one of us will make it but maybe we both will be fine. At this point I just want to rest and sleep and then we will be alert and then we can runs and the zombies will not gained up on us. Then I will be safe, and then what? I don't know I don't have the answers, and then we will safe. Ands what and then we will walks the streets and we will talked with ours friends and we will not have the military that were watched ours moved and then we would not have martial laws and soldiers and tanks on the streets eliminates the zombies. Then we can breathe easy and not worry that we would end being dead meat or becoming zombies with the infection, and I don't what is worst? Jimmy said too Kelly I just wants to be with my family and friends and being together and not separate again, I will never leave my family and go after that slut and lose my family, and then I loss Vicky and she became to be a zombie, and now I am alone and my family is gone forever. Because you went after the piece of ass and thought you were you were spent the rest of your life and then this happened? Yes you are right and I left Jenny to go after Vicky and then the virus hit and I was on journey of my life and I thought that I would not make it but you came along and you save, and I should thanks you! But we are not out of the woods so anything might happened and you still might died, and maybe I won't survive this epidemic, but the missiles will killed us, maybe even a bullet in the head. Please don't say that! I won't but we need to be quiet in here, yes I know the drill and let just be silent and then I can think and maybe find a cell phone and called someone and then they can comes and get us that is a good idea, well there are a lot of bad guys out there that they will robbed us, I know about that! The night came and the lights were out once in the while, Kelly flash the flashlight and watched Jimmy, and then Kelly fell asleep and about 5am Kelly heard a boom and then Kelly got up and the building cross street was burning and then tanks were coming near and Kelly said don't says a sound, ok I won't! then they heard they were marching through the city and one of soldier stop in front of the place that they were hiding out and then they left and Kelly was relief, and then about ten minutes the zombies were roaming the streets there were thousand and thousand of them, and Jimmy was really scare and frighten, and don't make a sound and I won't! Now it is time to go and he said are you crazy they are right outside and we need to go now because more will comes and then we will be trapped and I am not going, fine! But Jimmy refuse to go out of that building but he stayed and Kelly was inside the car and said come on, I am waiting for you but stay until the bunch of men that march into the city and Jimmy was getting himself out and one man pull out the gun and shot him in the head and then I knew that I need to leave now and I didn't wants to be tragic, and I started up the car and then I drove off speeding away and they were shooting at me and at the zombies. I did looked back and then I speeding away from there and those men were shooting the zombies and then I saw they were getting those men and there was no hope for them, they were perished in the battle there were too many zombies too killed, so I drove by the "Beverly center and I drove by Beverly boulevard, and then I decided too stop at the farmer market to pick some supplies and continue my journey to unknown areas , but I knew that I needed too get out of LA now and now I am headed to San Francisco, I knew that I had to cross the Golden Gate bridge and now I am headed on the 405, and I was not too far too the bridge but I saw a lot car on the side of the bridge but they were not there but I knew I had to cross over now. I drove slowly and makes sure that I wouldn't hit any car. But I makes many turns and looked out if no one was not standing there, and then I saw at my gas gauge and it was getting low and I didn't know if I was going to make it a cross. But I kept on driving, and driving, and I swerve toward the bridge and skid on side of the car and almost hit one and that was a close called. But I kept going until I got into the parking lot and parked the car and when inside the building and locked the doors and check each room and then I when inside one room that I felt it was secure and I step inside and locked the room and when on air to get some help! I started to speak and one heard me and kept saying please I am near the bay at a FM radio station would comes and gets me! I was plead and calling out for helps for hours and no one came to help me, and about two hours later, I heard a sound and I unlock the door and peek outside and it would the zombies. Now what will I do did I bring them here? Did they hears me went I was on air and then they heard me and what have I done! Once I started too speak and I said anyone can you near me I need your help and I am helpless in the radio station near the bay and it is not to far from the fish market and I wants need your help, immediately! Anyone hear me? I am near the fish market and I am alone and I need your helped I believe that the zombie's wants to make inside but please hurried, I don't wants to be dead meat. And no answered at alls and Kelly hid in the corner and make sure that the zombies were not sees her. Then Kelly heard someone knocking at the door of the studio, but Kelly looked and it was not a zombie, but it was the manager of the radio station and said what are you doing with my equipment? I am calling out for help. Don't touch the equipment, we need to contact someone and they need to save us, it too late, miss. Get out that room and you cannot kick me out, yes I can you are trespass; you cannot chase me out, to the zombies.

Are you out of your mind chasing me out, I will gets killed me. Get out of here now, no I am not going out, so I will steps with you, and he pull her out somehow Kelly slip back inside, then they grab him and torn him up into pieces, Kelly shut the door quickly, and put the chair near the door.

Now I feel safe but I am sole survivor, and I have no one to talking too me. Then Kelly sit back, thinking what will be my next move to stay or leave and I will stay for three days and the phone rang, and I wasn't sure to answers it… I better not. Two hours I went to the room and when online and hope that someone would called me, to my SOS called, but no one called. So Kelly once when to the doors and windows and check if it is locked and so she looked outside and they were standing around the building. I am surrounded, you hear from the zombies, I wants your brains, brain, brains, no then Kelly heard that the window broke and now Kelly locked in the " ON Air, and spoke in the microphone, please helped,, I am alone, and there are thousand of zombies at WSDF AM station near the bay, and but it was silent air. Kelly sat back, now what if sit here in silent and they will not hear me, please god let someone find me and I can be safe, about one hour later, Kelly fall asleep and then the door open and it the zombies, but Kelly doesn't realize, what happening at that moment of time. Suddenly Kelly wake up and saw them and now she doesn't have a place to runs, but somehow she manage to escape. Kelly ran too her van but realized it was out of gas and ran to another car that was locked and now Kelly kept on running and got into the back entrance of theatre, and close the door behind her. Kelly was relief, about being safe and but not having a weapons to defense herself. I don't even have a frigging to defense myself, but I need to search around and maybe they have some kind of weapon. Kelly search behind the counter and only find plastic forks and knives, shit, shit, shit, I am a goner! Then Kelly went into security and find a gun, and now I need to find bullets, and then she heard footsteps toward her and Kelly hid in the closet and waiting until the coast was clear,, and now Kelly was hearing we wants brains!!!! No one, how do I escape from her now? Kelly thought to herself and said I will go out of the back door that I came in, that is a good idea, now I am talking to myself. I must be crazy, but I did survive so far.

But I need to be quiet and so out in the front entrance now!

Land of the Dead

The zombies were everywhere and where I walks and I saw them, they followed me and they smelled and they wants to eat me up but I had no escape that this point, so I just tried not too be caught, and fight them off and so far I have the energy to beat them but some are much stronger and I don't if I have the strength and energy, anymore, but one thing I need to find a place and go there and locked myself inside tight. The night came and I was still standing on the street corner like bait, so what was I thinking, so I ran into the fish market and seen nothing unusually and I stay there and I watched the zombies roams the night.

I am the only one alive and I am hiding out in a fish market fish and they only smell fish and I think that the smell will helped me out, so far and I am safe but I don't know for how long, I know that I need to stay here until morning, but I know that I can stay here for forever but I need to find a vehicle and drive away and but I don't know where to do go? But I also knew that I cannot stay here neither, so do I just walks out and walks near the zombies with the fish smell and get into the red Chevy car and drive off, that is a plan said Kelly, but will it works? So now I need to sit tight and then, then wait until sunset and walks out the store and not too looked back. About ten minutes later, Kelly fell asleep and then she saw a cat coming toward her, she was not sure if the cat was infection or not but she didn't take any chances. Then she got up and walks way and then got a butcher knife and stabs the car and it was dead and then threw it out to the zombies. Zombies grabbed the cat and torn it into pieces and blood and parts on the street. Then Kelly quickly closed the door and sat down in the corner and prayed that someone were find her and were not be killed by the zombies. It is about three days later and Kelly said well I didn't leaves yet! I still feel safe and not threaten from the zombies but still Kelly was afraid what might be, and not what could happen too her. But Kelly was ready too having a battle with the zombies but fighting the zombies alone was being a losing battle. I am not ready too dies so I am staying here until I hears that they got rid of the zombies and the virus. Then Kelly notice that there was a TV in the back room of the store and I am going too sees what going on in the world right now. But the screen was blank and no reported about the zombies, and nothing. Then there was a special report, and it was saying things are going out of control and it is the land of the dead and leaves the city immediately, and go to the countryside and go to the green mountain in Utah and you will be safe, and Kelly thought how do I get there? But I need to leave San Francisco, and go to Utah, Green Mountain, that sounds like a peaceful town. So Kelly packs her bags with foods and her clothes and got her gun ready to shoot if needed for zombies and I don't think that they will notice me. Kelly step outside and walks around a hundreds zombies and got to the red Chevy car but at first it were not started and Kelly said, comes on start and need to get away but I need to cross the golden gate bridge and sees if there is anyone that were helped me. But I have a feeling that I am alone for awhile but I don't like being alone, with the land of the dead that control the streets that I uses too walks with my friends. Kelly said well now I am talking too myself and so I better stop and keeps driving and I sees that the Zombies are following me and I don't like it maybe I will get trapped and I will not be able to get out of this city. Then the car stall and said Kelly said shit, shit, shit, now what? I will get stomp by the zombies? I don't need this, not at alls. Then Kelly drove away and didn't looked back and thought to herself, the bridge crossing will be difficult and I don't know if I am going to make it this time around, I am not feeling right about that's ! But I have no choice and get to Utah and then I will be safe, I hope. Later that day went Kelly was about to cross the bridge the car stall and now she panic and thought to herself if the zombies were velour her and she were be into pieces and then Kelly thought I better stops thinking this ways. Kelly said I am the only sole survive and I need to find a cure and find other peoples can starts a new world without epidemic, but where is that world that I used too lives in? But life goes on and I just sit back and wait for someone to rescue me but now I need to find my way to Utah and not to get infection anyway I can. I will take one day at a times and I will make it too Utah and maybe there will be surviving there.

Now I will be crossing the bridge that is connect too Seattle and then I will be heading to Utah and I hope that I know where I am going, and I am out of foods and waters so I am just barely alive here! The sun is going down and the zombies will be coming in packs and I will not know what to do if they sees and I have no energy too fight them, so I will just give in and I will not suffer the pain of being alone, now I sound I am giving up, probably your right but I have no choice, do I? then Kelly thought and said no I am not going too let those zombies to eat me up, I will run but I will not know where to hide, and it is getting darker and darker and I don't sees what in front of me right now! But I still keeps on driving and I just hope that I leave the bridge without running into any zombies at this point, I will be relief but right now I am stress and I nervous, I am just lonely sole survive, just hoping for the next day too comes that I still live among the living but not the living dead, that I face everyday of my life, hope that you understand what I am going through, and it is a challenges. Now I am speaking loud and hope that everyone hears me but not the zombies of course, they were velour in a second and I were be there meal for the night! Now I am relief that I am off the bridge and in Seattle, and so far it seems that there are no zombies around I don't sees them, so far but I will not be careless and bump into one, that were be suicide for my part, so I just keeping driving and now looking for supplies for my journey too Utah, but the streets are empty and no one around that I don't sees anyone yet! I might just park the car and looked around for a while on Main street and then I will looked for some water and some foods in the grocery store across from the malls, and I will not walks too far from the car and I will tried not too get lost and easy way out if I need to. I walks and walks and so far no sight of zombies and I walks into the store and I thought it was clear but it was a old man with a shotgun and pointed at me and he looked into my eyes and said I thought you were a zombie but I sees that you are not so I will not shoot you, and Kelly said, so did have zombies here? Yes of course, you better hide, they will smell you and they will be saying we want your brains, but they will not get mind do you understand? Yes I do but don't worry mister; I know how to care of the zombies, I blast there head off and they are dead and so far I have not been bitten so I am not infection with the virus, about you? No but my family was taken from, me when I was not home the military took them and I never seen them again, I don't understand? Well, they had the symptoms of the virus and they took them to some Lab in LA and they never returned, so I am sorry what happened to them, and I cannot help you, but I can help you too fight and killed the zombies, and I am headed to Utah, oh! I see you are going to that camp and they will put you behind the fence and then killed you and burned you, well I am staying here, and I am going too waited for my family to welcome them home, and then we can be a family again! You know it not going too happened, and then he pushed her out of the door and said get out of here now!!! Kelly said are you crazy I need to stay here, no you don't you need to leaves now they will be coming soon!!! So Kelly walks toward the car and then she knew that the man was right and then I when inside the car and I drove away and about one minute later they storm into the fish market and torn him into pieces and he was dead, and they were eating his brains.. Kelly looked back and saw what was going on and left the street and heading too the highway and left the supplies behind at the fish market and Kelly was really upset and said now I will be staving and nothing and thirsty and I will dies. But Kelly kept on driving., and she spotted that she heard was bombs and missiles and a lot of shooting and now she knew that there was a battle going on and she were probably be in the middle of the battle. Kelly then thought well maybe I should go back and then she said no I am going too sees what going on there! Went Kelly got there, there was a barrack that she couldn't go through but thought maybe she were just climb over and then said that must be a bad idea, wait a minute I need to decided what to do about going to a Las Vega, so do cross or what? Well I will go there and I have many days to go to Utah and I think I will just sneak in and no one will notice me, that am a plan, said Kelly. Ok what do I do now? Yes I know I will just climb over and sneak into the jeep and sit there and hide in the back seat of the jeep and no one will know that I am there! Stops for a moment!

No Place too hide

Kelly walks very quiet and Kelly thought that the military was there but there was a surprise for Kelly, that Kelly when inside the camp of Zombies, and Kelly hid for hours and hours and then she looked out and saw them and she said what have I done? Am I so stupid that I went into a place that I were be trapped and eaten up, so I need to get back too my car and not being seen by anyone and especially not the zombies. What do I do, the solider might shoot me in my head and they think that I am a zombies, how careless did do? No, no, no, I just wander if the jeep was started up and I break through those fences and then I will be freeing the zombies, and that is not a good idea, and now I am trap.

Well, I have a plan so I will just squeeze through the wire and fit in and then I will go through and no one will notice me and I will just gets into my jeep and then I will drive away and go head to Las Vega near the Golden Nugget casino and sees who inside and I probably should check out when I gets there, so will alls the street be barbwires, I hope not! So far everything seems fine, and suddenly a saw a Silver Honda that just almost hit me so I just curve the opposite direction. I almost crash through the glass window of the building and stops the jeep, and ran out and said don't you sees where you were going, are you blind? No I am not but you were on my ways and you cause the accident. Miss you did I was first on the road and now my jeep is damage and I need to gets away from here. Well are you going to take me, I will be stuck and I cannot stay here alone, so I guess you coming with me and it will be nice to have company, well I will be bad company, sorry about hitting you but it was dark and I didn't sees you coming, so I forgive you. But don't do it again, fine, I won't! so

Kelly jump into the car and then what is your name, it is Roger and I lives not too far from here and would like too comes to my house? No I was heading toward Las Vega and some placing are roads are blocks and I need to get too Las Vega too the Golden Nugget casino and sees what was going on, beside the zombies invaded, that true! Maybe the military might clear roads the road block and we will be able to go inside the city and sleep in one of the hotels? That was being nice. Yes it was be. So let go and find out what happening there, I am game and I have nothing too do, just help damsel distress, no I am not stop saying that's! Stop teasing me, ok I will! They both were silent alls the ways too Las Vega. Then Kelly said too Roger why did you go there and why did you save me and someway tried too killed me? You are asking too many questions and I don't have the answers to those questions. Thanks for being honest, Roger. I tried too being but I am not prefect but I try my best and so I will tell about myself. Well I am from LA and I had family there, and I used too worked at the lab, where I make the antidote, and then the outbreak. So you probably started the virus and you are in the middle of it, well you might be right! But I do wants to fix and I don't have a clue but I will tried my best, but I am type that solve problem but sometime it just don't works neither, I do understand Kelly, thanks Roger you being so nice too me. Well, I guess I am in a good mood but we must be prepare how we will deal with zombies and now I am not alone and I thought I was but I also lose someone too the zombies and I don't wants to get too close too anyone until the crisis are over, I agree with you, said Roger to Kelly. We are about two miles away from the casino and I will parked in the garage and I think we should be safe, I did that and I done that somehow I ran into zombies in that situations, well maybe they are gone, I hope so! About ten minutes later, Roger went inside the garage and parks the car and said "let go into the elevator" yes and make sure you know what floor that we are parked for an easy escape, good ideas. They both inside and push the button down and to the lobby of the Golden Nugget casino, and they steps into the lobby and they looked around and so far seems too be clear and then Kelly said looks! What are you seeing; I think that we are not alone here! You are right but we need to leave, I want to sees how my luck is! I will put ten dollars into the machine and maybe I will win a jackpot, so who were paid you? Good question, Kelly, yes no fooling around with the slots, fine. Roger did put the money and started to plays the "wild cherry" and so far didn't hit anything but then the last spin, and then he hit five grand and then the zombies came and Roger said about the money, well I never had five grand., make your choice? Your life or money, maybe I can have both what you think, I would choose my life. Fine, I guess you were rich, no but enough to live on and that alls, and I was happy, and now I just think if the crisis were end. I hope so a lot of peoples die from this virus and also it is like a land of the dead. Yes it is and I want to be safe and being loved like once and how do I change this I don't know, but there are too many too killed. It is out of control, the situation, is worst each day of ours lives, yes I know. But now we need to find a place to stay for awhile and Kelly said maybe we should stay at the mirage and Roger agree and we will take the penthouse, and the zombies will not get us, but we need to find an escape route. That is true, and let go and we will get some supplies and stay quiet and we will be enough, went we gets rescue that day will comes, that is true and I like how you think, Roger. They left the golden nugget and when to the mirage and park on the upper level and parked the car and when into the lobby and got a key too one of the penthouse and then Kelly got the foods and waters, and then they both inside and when up to the penthouse and locked the elevator too prevent the zombies to enter, and they knew that they were secure, now. We will be able too sees what going on and we have a helicopter and the keys in case and we are secure, good to hears. Now we can relax but not off guard, yes I do. Now Kelly and Roger getting closer and closer, and Roger kissed her lips and then Kelly said what are you doing? You are so attractive and I think that I love in love with you. Do you feel about me the same? I am sure, but I do feel something but not exactly what? I don't wants to fall in love with you and then the zombies comes and bite you and then you will be gone and I cannot deal with that's! Fine, do you like me? Yes I do and I don't want to lose you, you won't! You cannot promise me, I can, I will not let the zombies get me. No, one not even me and I know that's! So let stops talking about it and then let get closer, ok! So Roger grabbed her and holds her tight and then kissed her lips and said you make me happy and that why I save you, I feel for you went I took you out of your car, well I step out of the car, yes that what I meant. Fine, so you wants to have sex with me, no I wants to make love with you, so that night they got together and then they make love all night long!!! They spent time looking out of the window and they only saw was that the population of the zombies grew, and Kelly said we will not able to go outside, we can go on the rooftop and stay there for awhile but we will unlocked the elevator and that is not good, yes we will take some risk, but we will be fine, just trust me Kelly, I do! Kelly and Roger it was about one week and then it was a month and then it was like five years in the penthouse and then Kelly notice that she heard gun fire and then bomb blowing up and then saw soldiers marching on the streets with rifles, and then Kelly woke up Roger and said there is something going on!!! I heard that sound, and it seems like a battle, of some kind. What do we do? Now, I think we should stay here and not too make sound, and they will not shoot us and think that we were zombies. don't worry I will tried to called them from my cell phone and tell them that we are not zombies and we are not infection and Kelly said probably that not a good idea, why do you says that's? I when through the military and I had a bad experience and I don't wants to do it again! I do understand but we need to tells them, no we don't we just stay here! Fine, we have bigger chances of being shot if we don't says anything at alls so you disagrees with me but I am going to called them, fine but don't tell them that I am here, just in case, ok I won't! If they storm into this room I will hide and I will find you, when they take you too the zombies camp for experience. You will be "test lab" they will poke you and give you shots and then they will sees if you have the gene for the virus, and if you do they will use you like a test you and tested non stop, well maybe I should be quiet and don't make the called. Right choice, I am happy that you will not say anything. Do you think that they will leave and we can just stay here, well now we need to stay in the dark and no lights, just sit and be quiet, Roger. You need to know the drill and not be notice by the military, good rules, Kelly. That why you survive so long and didn't get caught and the military did not test you has lab rat? Yes, good job Kelly to keep me alive, but we are not out of the woods but we still need to deal with the zombies.

Thin Ice Zombies IN LA
Nowhere to runs or hide
Battle!

The Battle

Kelly looked out and then saw the zombies was coming from one from one direction and then another direction that the soldiers were marching toward the zombies they came closer and closer. Kelly said the zombies seem they are growing and then soldiers seem like they are out numbered and that is not good for us, and we will not be able to go out there! But Kelly said well, this might be a chance to get weapons and then and helped them out. I don't know if we are going too make it and the zombies are more powerful and not weak and they are strong and they pull one solider into tiny parts, and they just want too eat the brain.

The virus is infection does something in the brain and I think it shut it down and then it burst the vessel in your brain and then you died and then somehow you wake up and you wants to eats brains non stops.

How do you know this knowledge, because I make the antidote and then but the antidote does not have nothing to do with the virus. But what does and how do we prevent of spreading, right now we have no choice and so we have to stay inside and if we do outside we will get infection by the virus and we will become zombies. It is a face off between zombies and the soldiers and it really looked bad. I don't what will happened but I says that we need to stay here and shut off the AC and don't let no air inside at this moment and it is very vital, do you understands Roger, because it live or death, so I think that I choose life.

Did you close all the vents and everything that were protection us and yes I did and no one will make us sick. Yes I do know that about keeping things out and not letting them in, and that how I was not infection at the farm, because I knew that I had to hide in the water well and it was secure, and you make it out alive,, yes, yes. So why you go out there and listens what they are saying about the progress about killing off the zombies, I am not going out there! I am not going too get shot in the head neither. Well someone has too do a looks out and then we will be able to go the garage and gets away if it is not road block and it were be terrible and we would end up getting killed in the process, and that were not be good. I don't wants that and I don't neither so I just sit here in the penthouse and I am not going out and letting them up here, ok for now we will stay here, and if thing change we will have to move quickly. Do you understand, yes, and it will not be easy, I also understand what you are saying but the zombies are defeated the soldiers and that is bad and we will be stuck here for awhile, yes and we are running out of supplies and one of us we need to go out there and somehow and it will be difficult and you know your ways around here? Not exactly said Kelly I been here before and things have change here, and some doors are that been opened now they are shuts. But we need to find the tunnels that lead to the underground and there we will be safe from the battle of the nuclear missiles that they will used if the soldiers are outnumbered, and I know but the chance of getting radioactive, and the poisonous in the air and burned our skins and even worst. I don't want to think about it. But we are grantee too make it alive. But sure hell I am going to tried and no one will stop me and I am going to beat the odd, I know you did. But we need to leave tonight through the tunnels underneath the mirage casino and head to the seaport and take a boat and sail too Bahamas, and sit in the sun and it will be good to be out and not worry about the zombies. But we don't know if they are there too. But they are still fighting the battle and I think we should pack ours stuff and leaves now went we have the chance Roger and don't says no! I am ready and I am going to open the elevator secure elevator that we stay for a long time and not sure what going happened, and we will try too not to failure, our mission. But we won't said Kelly, I been in a few and I did make it out and I am not going to think negative thought at this time and then they got inside the elevator and when down and instead to the roof. But Roger was silent and worries what might happen at this point. "They both steps out and then looked around and they were headed to the basement." Looked out Roger it is coming toward you and I will and they both step inside and blot the door locked and walks very quickly downstairs and they reach the bottom of the stairs through the kitchen there was a passage way through a secret door that took them into the tunnels to reach the outside of Las Vega and a car was there and they didn't know that's until they got there! Wow we are lucky and hope that the car will start up and we can leave this awful place. So Roger and Kelly sat in the car and it start up and they left that place and also they heard sounds of zombies. Can you believe it that zombies were following us and we still cannot get rid of them? But now we have a chance and to drive away from sin city and head to the coast and get on a boat and sail away. That is a nice dream, but it will happen. Now Kelly said that I will take a snooze and I tell me when we reach the dock and tell me that we have no fear of zombies, I will tried but I will not promise, ok I do totally understand you what you are saying. Are you saying that we are going back to LA from Las Vega, yes and we will take a boat on the Pacific Ocean and head to Bahamas? Yes and are you sure that there are no zombies there? I am not sure but we are going there! But we need to go through the zombies before we get to the shipyard and then we can get any boat and sail the sea, yes! I cannot wait to leave this infestation and go where we can relax and not worry about the zombies that are true. Not sure, if it spread alls over the world, so you are saying that the zombies probably are everywhere. Yes that what I am saying stop talking negative, Roger to Kelly. Well I just want the life to be back too normal, probably will never happen again, stop it! It wills you need to have faith, and hope and it will happen, fine! We are very near the boat that we will sails; I cannot wait to sail away!

"White House invaded by Zombies"

"Special Report" the white house got broke in by zombies, and the first family not secure area unknown areas and the vice president and his family been taken by the zombies at the west wing of the white house.

"President Oliver was advice to go the shelter, and refuses to leave his wife and children behind, and massive bodies in the front lawn of the white house, and then Kelly said did you hear that special report. No I am focusing about finding the boat and sail away from here. That what we are doing and the president can deal with his problem, that is right!

Then the news is saying, that they cannot find his wife and children and the white house got slaughter and so that is not good at alls. Then there a martial law and virus is spreading and then President said that everyone to find a safe shelter, keeps your door locked and then it when off air and nothing, this is really shit, going on!!! No kidding so I sees a boat that we can takes, and go and go and sees them are coming toward us, shoot at them. They got to the dock and parked the car and then walks up to the boat and then Roger said I cannot find the keys to started up the boat so we have a problem and they are coming closer and gaining up on us and then I find the key and he started up and they backup and move and into the water and sail away and now Kelly relief. Now Kelly just sat on the top of the deck and looked at the coast of California, ands the news alert, the President and his family are safe and no one got injury of the zombies that broke into the white house and President Oliver is safe. That is a relief, yes it is when this virus is over, hope that the President will care and help the injury peoples, after this battle between the night of the living and the living and hope that no one occurs don't occur again! back at the while house, at the doorway and entrance of the white lays the secret services slaughter and the zombies roaming the white house and meanwhile the President has a decision too make is too push the nuclear bombs into alls the city of the USA, and his wife Marty said you cannot do this because my family is out there and they could be alive and don't send those bombs, I am begging for my family in North Carolina, I won't right now but it I need too I will,, do you understand? Yes I do but promise me that you won't Billy! Fine I will not and I don't know how long we need to stay here in the shelter. Back with Kelly and Roger and Kelly lying on the deck and said do you know where you're going? Yes, are you sure? Two hours, the president heard a knock at the shelter and His wife Marty should we looked and sees who there? I am not sure at this point. Just be quiet and we will be all right!! Sir, sir are you alls right! Can you opened the door and I need to gets inside now, they are coming near, so are you going to let him in? No he might be infection and he was shouting and screaming and then the zombies came and grabbed and then Bill said well I think that he is fine and left, how could you let one of your worker too get killed? He know that is job is dangerous, Bill you have changed and yours sons will sees how you are treating your peoples and that is a bad example, no it is not and I am President. Yes you are but I had no choice in the matter and so many innocent peoples are dead and we are in shelter and safe, and then the lights when off and then the secure door opened and what happened? I don't know what happen don't let the zombies sees you, but didn't you say that they can smell you? Yes but boys hide into the walls and you and your mother will checks out the halls don't comes out until I tell you do? Yes dad but we wants to go with you are very scares here and it is dark so here is a flashlight but don't lights it up too much because it will attract the zombies, ok we won't! So Marty and Bill check out the halls and seem too be clear and then Marty said why don't we get the boys and leaves this place and I know that you know how to fly a helicopter and so just could fly away! so I will get the boys and so we can leave and we will meet you at the back lawn, but I am sure if it is secure, but we need to go and we need to go now, understand? Yes I do but I am not sure is a good idea, Marty. Bill and Marty approach the shelter and Marty flash and called out too her sons and then Marty got closer and one of her son bite her and she fell to the ground and then Bill called out Marty where are you, I am waiting for you and ours sons, and then the little son came up too his dad and gave him a hug and then bite him on the neck and the President was on the floor and dead, and about thousand of zombies roamed the "white house".

Then the latest news alert that the President was slaughter in the white house and the virus spread alls over to Europe and island and Bahamas, and now what we just sit at sea and have no home at alls, said Kelly too Roger, I guess so. I don't like this, looked they are even in the water, and we are not on land and they are following us, no I cannot believe this not at alls. What will happen to our country that we don't have a president, well after the endemic probably will have election, I hope so? So the president and his family perish in the "white house" and that is terrible, I know and that alls I can says, the world might end, and but someone has to survive. So we will build soon has they elimination the zombies and we will have new world. That is a nice dream, you have Kelly. I know it will happen and I know that I will not go back to my job never again! but now you are saying that's but I believe that you will go back and get a raise and forget what happen in the past, never I will always remember what happen to my family and friends that perish in the battle of zombies.

I don't wants too talked about it anymore, and looked Roger they are standing on the others side of shore and I am not sure that we should go to land until it is safe to do so! Your right! I need to agree with you this time, but I am sure that "battle" will continue, even though the new world will comes, you are saying that we will never gets rid of the zombies? Yes that what I am saying, there are too many too killed. The latest report that the "white house" is burning and no survivor to be seen and it is a tragedy to the "America family perish and further detail will be coming and there are battle in the streets and the soldiers are being defeated by the zombies, and then it got silent and a blank screen, and now I think the news peoples got hit by the zombies that is terrible, I know. So let says a little pray for the Peoples that are fighting the zombies that were creative by the government, that is true, and that was there fatal mistake that they made. But there are more zombies and the soldiers are turning into zombies and we don't have a world to lives and now what we just sail and find a location non zombies zone, well I don't know if that place exist I think that is only an fantasy world these days and we will runs out supplies and we probably will dies anyways, I don't wants to your nonsense and you are making me sick. Well I am speaking the truth and I don't want you too denied it; Kelly but this are the facts what going on in the world and you know that the President didn't survive and how will we. We must lives, one thing I don't give up and how many battles that you been and you still wants to fight still and I don't have the strength and the energy to fight. I still wants to fight and sees my friends and my family but they are alls gone and now I just wants to make it too the next day! Kelly called out to Roger do you sees the smoke in the trees on that island? Yes I do and what do you think that they are surviving and they are giving a SOS to gets rescue, it is possibility, I think that we should go there and sees if they need our help, ok but if zombies pop up we are leaving immediately, see I agree, said Kelly so let go now!!! They took the little boat and landed on the island and said be careful and watched your steps, well so far go good, and then Kelly and Roger and walks and walks further into the woods from the beach and then Kelly saw a little boy and he was drool that came from his mouth and bloody hands and saying "I wants brains, and Kelly said I guess that is the clue too go back to the boat and sail away, you are probably right! But don't you see that we are surrounded by the zombies, so did you bring the rifles and the bullets? No I left them on the boat so we need to just go through them and don't get bitten, easy to says, went you are in this situation, just great! Kelly. Kelly and Roger were fighting off the zombies and then Kelly said they are coming out of the water, so we cannot go back too the boat and we need to runs and hide in the cave, are you nuts they could be there and I am going back to the boat, don't Roger I advice not too! But where do we runs too get give me a hint right now!! Fine, just follows me and we will go inside and then we will wait until morning. Then we will go back to the boat and then we will head back to the west coast and then we will called someone and find out if it end of the virus and did it stop. There could be someone that could tell us but the only thing that I see are those "ZOMBIES" everywhere and seems like no escape, do you know what I am saying?

Yes, I do and we will be fine, just hold me tight! I will, Kelly.

Island Zombies

So they walks into the cave and then they used the some bushes cover the cave and then we need to be quiet, and then we need not to start a fire and then we just can be silent and make sure that they don't get inside so we are only protection by the bushes, they just can walks in when we are inside and then eat us up and we turned into zombies. Well you wanted too comes here, and I had a bad feeling about this place and I don't know if we are going to make it back to the boat in the morning. I don't know if we have a fighting chance to make it alive so let me make love too you tonight!! Yes I want to be in your arms and I do love you so much and we might be the last survivor and we need to build new world, if that exist, well I don't know... Roger held Kelly in his arms all night long and out sounds that they heard were, I smell fresh meats and I want yours brains, and brains in front of the cave, and Roger snuck out for a second and they were standing there! now what maybe there is a other ways out I hope so, I don't have the strength to runs anymore said Roger, and I am staving, and hungry and thirsty, so am I, and I don't know if we are going to find some kiwi or papaya to eat on this island, well I saw some spring water near the waterfalls near the beach, so maybe we should get some maybe,, not sure. Not right now but I will quietly go there alone and I will be right back, you are not leaving me alone, do you understand? Yes I do and I am not staying alone and if something happen too I and I will be alone. I am coming with you but it is easier too travel alone and you might distract them and they will follow us, no I won't! you think that you will leave me alone and go back to the boat and now you acting paranoid, no I am not I been alone before I am staying behind but coming along.

I am behind of you and I am not holding you back, but walk a bit faster, I am close to you so far, I am a inches away, oh I sees the fruits and lets pick some up and so how can I carry them? Well in your hands, but too many, to hold, so I will go back and gets more lately, fine. Don't you see them coming, no I don't! They are headed toward us and we don't have no place hide and so jump into the bushes and then Roger jump behind her and then be quiet, I am. They are passing by and I think they won't hear we and then we can sneak into the cave and then we can eat.

Looks so many passing us and when they do just get out of bushes and runs to the cave and don't looked back and I will sees you at the cave soon, I promise Kelly, take my word. I won't be long and make sure they don't sees you and don't worry about me I will be fine! About one hour Kelly was waiting at the cave and Kelly looked out and didn't sees no sight of Roger and now she was about to steps out he came back and Kelly was relief and said I was planning to find you and Roger said I have a plan to get us out of here,, but how Roger, well used night vision, so where do we find that? I find a house south of the beach and we will be able to stay there and I also saw guns and dynamite and a lot of bullets. So where are the peoples I didn't sees them but they can shoot us, that is true and maybe they are zombies, and about one minute later, do hears what I am hearing, what is that sounds, it sound bats, what? You must be kidding, no I am not! This island has bat and zombies and that is not good for us, I agree that why we need to get those weapons and leaves this island immediately, I do understand, I know how to deal with the LA Zombies and but with zombies here not sure and what else is infection luring the woods. We need to go to the house and leave this place I agree, so show me where the house is and is it far from the beach? Yes, will it be a problem getting back to the boat, I don't have answers for you but without weapons and we will not survive, well I am willing to take a chance, me too, so let go now and the sooner we get the weapons and the sooner we get away, yes. I will follows you and then we can get back to the boat and then one bat over my head and almost bit me and I said we need to hide these bats are hungry and they don't looks like normal species of bats and they have a strange odor and what are you saying they are zombies/ vampires and more powerful, you must be kidding, I am not joking and I am serious and we need too hurried. I do hear you, loud and clear. About five hour day Roger and Kelly walking through the woods and then they final reach the house and then Roger open the door ands said it is clear and we can go inside and Kelly said I need to sit down and I am exhausted so am I. Kelly sat down and then she saw a lady step into the living room and said what are you doing in my house? Well, my friend Roger, told me about this place but you need to take me off this island, yes I will and Roger came into the room, so are you ready to go now, "please take me" so what is your name? Tina and my son, Brian, and he is a little sick and what wrong with him, he just not feeling well and he drool a lot and Kelly said he is infection and I need to give a shot of antidote, will it helped him? So how many days did he was sick? About a week, no the shot will not help Brian, he will turned into zombies soon. I don't believe you Kelly give him a chance to get better, no I cannot he will turned, I am not going to leave him, come on Roger we need to go now and Tina said wait for me, but your son cannot comes. You must take us and I will watched him, my son is the only relative that I have alive, so Roger pick him up and said I am going take him to the boat and Kelly said make sure that he doesn't bite you or drool on your hands, that will infection you, thanks! Tina follows them and they were near the beach and no zombies, good timing, and they alls when on the boat and sail to the bigger boat and sail away from the island, and then they saw the zombies standing on the island, that was a close called. Yes it was.

Moon Eclipse

Kelly and Roger and Tina and Brian were on the boat and they were sailing back to LA, and suddenly it got dark, and Kelly said what going on? I think it is "moon eclipse" that occurs and then it wake up more zombies, and she looked at her son, and I think he is sleeping, and Kelly touch him and he was cold has ice, and she tried to tell Roger that soon they will have too shoot the zombie on the boat and at first he didn't understand what she was saying and a minute later he woke up and was about to bite, Tina, Kelly shoot him in the head and Tina said you bitch you killed my son, he was fine and now he is dead and your going to pays for it, your son was a zombie and he about too bite you, you are a fucking liar, and a bitch. I save your life and you are calling me names, you whore. This thanks that you gave me, now I am alone, no you are not you have us and we are a family, but I am not with her, with you, Roger. Girls, girl, behave I cannot deal with tense and then with the zombies too.

I know what you mean but I need to be not nerve wreck and you killed my son, and he was my baby, how would you feel if it was your son? I don't wants to talked about it now, so let beat those zombies and get home I agree, we too. So Roger was losing his cool and then said to Kelly you easy making enemy and you are ready to fight and you don't care who you hurt but you wants too be the best what you do and you don't want anyone to be in your ways! Yes, yes and what do you wants from me? I just wants to be home and with my family but I have loss my dad during the battle and then now we have too be careful that they don't chew us up and eat our brain, that really terrify me and I don't want to be dead meat, I don't neither, and especially the moon eclipse, and the dead walks and the population grows and we are in really trouble, no kidding said Tina, you shot my son and you are going to paid for it, for saving your life. I don't need that kind of thanks but I really missing my son and how he is gone with the infection that your lab made,, but it is not my fault so, don't accuse me, there were much more evil persons working at the lab, well you were one of them, probably once and then the "breakout" I started to helped out the infection peoples and gave them the antidote, so I am not that bad. I had no choice when I got the job I thought I was helping but I cause the spread of the virus that somehow got into the water and foods and probably now it is airborne, you think it is airborne? Yes I do! Well when I was working in the lab the vent were opens and that how it got spreads and a lot of peoples dies. "watched out they are boarding the boat and they going to bite us…no said Tina and one the zombies was so close that Kelly manage to shoot it in the head. Tina said you almost got me and I am lucky too be alive, yes you are don't argue and you get really means and so I don't wants to talks with you so Tina said just went downstairs and shut the door behind her.

Then Kelly said let us in, what are you doing nothing! Why you just open the door and let us in, said Kelly and Roger and friends and what are you doing? Well I am just relaxing and thinking when we get to LA, I will go to the police and tell them that you killed my son. Well I should have you gets bitten by your son and then I would have shot you in the head and I were have peace, you bitch,, don't called me names and I will threw you off the boat and let the zombies eat you up,, I dare you, girly, what do you think that you are better than I am? Roger said stops bickering, and I will shut you both up, I am the only that fighting off the zombies and you two bitches did not lift a finger too help me. That is a lies and I don't want you says that is not the truth, Roger, I helped you out and you almost got bitten a few times, is that true, Roger? Not sure, be truthful, well ok that is the truth and Kelly is a survivor of 2006 in LA and still beaten them and killing each zombies she meets, that true, yes! But Tina didn't comes out but was shouting out of from the downstairs and then Kelly broke the window and got inside and unlock the door and said, missy, you cannot stay here because it is Roger and my bedroom and you will have to stay upstairs,, that is unfair bitch, I told you don't called me bitch again, I will threw you into the water, with the zombies, so you are threaten me, not exactly? Roger said looks at the moon eclipse, I am and I don't believe it and the moon looked like blood in the moon, I don't know what you are saying, and but I do, you must be high on some drug, you are some crazy lady to says that too me, and I don't like you at alls. Just listens and we need to get along to survive, do you understanding? Yes I will I do want to live, I am glad you girls have agreement, me too. So they sat down and talked and then hug each others, and they would mad at each others, and Roger, was happy now. Tomorrow we will be home and we will check out the Beverly center, and sees if clear of zombies. I hope so, me too. The moon eclipse passing and the sun came out, they were heading the dock of LA, Kelly was relief, and then they heard guns shooting, and smoke in air, building burning, and peoples on ground torn into pieces and body parts, bloods and parts, on the streets of LA, no we need to turned back we cannot stay here, but why the ZOMBIES ARE COMING. What? Don't you see them? Yes I do, so the battle continue and we need to sail away, now, "WE Wants Brains, brains, brains, no, they ran to the boat and said we need to go away until the battle end,, but the zombies are defeated us, and we need to go now!!! Yes, remove the rope and then they sail off into the sunset. The Battles continue and there is no end, yet, continue BATTLE....with Zombies and Humans... Continue battle...

About the Author

Jean Marie Rusin, lives with her mom and brother in New Britain, Conn. And Member of the Connecticut Authors and Publishers Association, and Jean Marie Rusin, Graduation from Connecticut School of Broadcasting on September 7, 2007, and Jean Marie Rusin, has her own talk radio on blogtalkradio.com and Jean Marie Rusin, also on Face books and twitter and myspace.com and my website is www.jeanmarierusin.com